ool
co   to
go   ke
a   ed
ou   It
wa   ut
th

                                                                    p-
po

                                                                    ?"
Jo

                                                                    a
co

                                                                    se
hi   ly
wo   ly
couldn't stop himself. He'd show them. He would
give these cruel kids a Halloween "treat" they
would never forget. . . .

SCREAMERS™

THE FRIGHT MASK
& Other Stories to Twist Your Mind

by Don Wulffson

Rainbow Bridge®
Troll Associates

10 9 8 7 6 5 4 3 2 1

CONTENTS

THE FRIGHT MASK

*T*he loneliness was gnawing at Billy's insides. All he wanted to do was fit in with his classmates. But the kids at Humaine Middle School were just like the kids at all the other schools he had attended over the years. They didn't seem to want any part of him. He was a runt. A loser. An outsider. He was always one of the last ones to get picked, if he got picked at all, to play basketball, or baseball, or handball. And when invitations for parties were given out, it seemed there was never one for him.

It was always hard for Billy to take, but tonight it was especially hard. Tonight was Halloween. Billy had asked several kids—Brad Kelly, Josh Steinberg, Marie Kennedy, and Pete Cortez—if they wanted to go trick-or-treating with him, but the most he had got was a maybe from Josh. Marie had just laughed in his face, Brad Kelly had given him a flat-out no, and Doug had told him to get lost.

Feeling lost already, Billy now headed home from school through the streets of Lafayette, Pennsylvania. It wasn't much different from all the other towns he had lived in as a kid. His parents, both scientists employed by the government, had literally moved around the world, and Billy had to go with them. Their work involved doing tests on soil, water, plant, and animal samples from places all over the globe, so moving had simply become second nature for them.

It was harder for Billy. He repeatedly was faced with the not-so-easy task of trying to fit in at a new school, and the kids at Humaine were proving to be just as mean to newcomers as the kids in all the other towns.

Walking up Braemore Lane, Billy tried to get out of his foul mood. But by the time he got home, he still had a sour expression on his face.

"What's the matter, Billy?" his mom asked the minute he clomped dejectedly through the front door. She obviously had been working in the back room where she and Billy's dad kept the soil samples. She wiped dirt from her hands with a paper towel and looked at him with concern. "You look upset, dear."

"It's Halloween, Mom," Billy moaned, plunking himself down on the sofa. "I want to go trick-or-treating with the other kids, but no one wants to go with me. And besides, I don't even have a costume!"

"Well, it's not too late," his mother said soothingly. "I'm sure I could make something for you in time for tonight."

Billy's dad was standing in the doorway, holding a large plant in rubber-gloved hands. "This whole Halloween bit has always seemed a little silly to me," he said. "Still, I understand how important it might be for someone your age."

"What sorts of things are the other children going to be wearing?" asked his mother.

"Oh, you know, they'll dye their hair and wear all sorts of masks and put false fangs in their mouths. You know, the usual. But I don't have anything like that."

Suddenly his father broke into a wide grin. "I have an idea!" he said. "Why don't you go as what you are every day? Go as a normal everyday boy."

"Great idea," exclaimed his mom with a laugh. "It'll be *your* joke on *them*!"

"I don't know, Mom," Billy said. "We'll understand the joke, but I don't think the kids will. They'll just think I couldn't come up with anything."

"But don't you see, Billy?" his dad said encouragingly. "*They're* the ones who'll be wearing the same old Halloween outfits. *You'll* be the one wearing something original."

Billy broke into a grin. "You know, you're right, Dad. And you, too, Mom. The joke *will* be on them, and if they're too dumb to get it, then that's their problem."

"That's the spirit," his dad said with a hearty laugh. He gave Billy a pat on the back, then headed into the back room to continue his work.

Later that evening, as soon as it got dark, Billy grabbed a shopping bag to fill with goodies and walked into the living room to say good-bye to his parents.

"You'll be a real hit!" his dad said with a grin.

His mom gave him a big hug. "Now, be careful, Billy," she said. "Be careful of cars, and also of pranksters. And remember: kids can be mean. If they don't get the idea behind your costume, don't let it bother you."

"I won't, Mom," Billy said, putting on a brave front to

reassure her. "I just hope they'll let me explain my costume before they put it down."

"I'm sure they will," his mom said, giving him another hug. And with that Billy was off to try to find some other trick-or-treaters to hook up with.

But after tromping along through the cold, dark streets for a while, a familiar lonely, empty feeling gradually began to gnaw at Billy. True, his mom and dad had made him feel happy and secure, but now he was all alone, with no one to turn to. Worse, he felt genuinely spooked. The streetlights of Lafayette were old and weathered. The glass was yellowed by age, and it cast a sick amber glow over the neighborhood, like light strained through egg yolk. At almost every house candles flickered inside the carved-out orange skulls of pumpkins, making them look almost alive, and dogs yapped at all the trick-or-treaters scurrying from door to door. It was hard for Billy to be out alone on any night, but on Halloween it was twice as hard . . . and scary, too.

Finally Billy spotted a troop of ghosts, goblins, and vampires rushing up the walkway of a house across the street. He followed them, hoping to join their group.

For a moment Billy blended in, sticking out his bag to receive a handful of candy from a lady who pretended to be afraid. But after the door shut and the group headed down the walkway, someone noticed him.

"Who's the nerd?" said a muffled voice from behind a rubber Frankenstein mask.

A fake skeleton poked Billy in the ribs. "Nobody asked you to tag along."

Another kid jumped at Billy with his fingers outstretched like claws. "Boo!" the boy, dressed as a zombie, shrieked at Billy.

Startled, Billy jumped back and fell into a hedge. The others laughed and walked away.

"Who was that?" Billy heard somebody in the troop say as they hurried up the street.

"Oh, he's that new kid in school," answered Frankenstein. "A creep named Billy somebody-or-other."

Scratched and sore, fighting back tears, Billy struggled out from the hedge. For a moment he thought of just returning home. But his parents would be upset and worried that he wasn't fitting in. *No*, he decided, *I'm going to stick it out! I'm not going to be a quitter.*

Just then a lady passed by holding the hands of two little girls, both dressed up as fairy princesses.

"Hi," said Billy, picking off bits of the broken hedge. "Happy Halloween."

The woman mumbled something, and pulling the little princesses closer to her, hurried past Billy as though he were some sort of dangerous weirdo.

Forlorn, Billy made his way along the street, hoping to see another band of trick-or-treaters who might let him join them.

Soon he spotted a werewolf, two football players, and a cyclops cheerleader scooting across the lawn of a house. They were all running and laughing and seemed to be having a great time, their bags stuffed full of treats. He started to call out to them, but one of them recognized him and yelled, "Hey, there's Billy! What's the matter, Billy? Were you too stupid to think of a costume?"

Billy just looked at his shoes and turned away. *Oh, well*, he thought. *Even if I can't hook up with a group of kids, at least I can get lots of candy. I'm not going to make a total waste of Halloween.*

Resigned to going trick-or-treating alone, he went to a few houses by himself. Most people just looked him up and down, smiled weakly when he said he was dressed as a "boy," then tossed a candy bar or some other treat into his sack.

At the next house Billy decided to make growling noises and say that he was a "wild boy." Happy with his new idea, he rang the bell and the door swung open. A little boy in a pumpkin costume peeked out from behind his father. "How come he doesn't have a costume, Daddy?" the little boy asked, looking up at his dad with big blue eyes.

"I *do*," said Billy, smiling. "I'm a—"

"No, you don't," said the little boy. "You just have ordinary clothes on and you aren't even wearing a mask."

"Don't be rude, Teddy," said the man, dropping a candy bar into Billy's sack. "Sorry, young man," he told Billy and softly shut the door.

For a moment Billy just stood there. From behind the door he heard voices. "But *why* couldn't he at least wear a mask?" Billy heard the little boy ask his father.

"Maybe he can't afford a costume," the father said. "Maybe he just wasn't into the spirit of Halloween."

Fighting back tears, Billy hurried from the house. *I am into the spirit of Halloween,* he thought, wandering around aimlessly, a scowl on his face. *I just don't like being into it alone.*

He looked in his treat bag. There were only a few things in it. It would be embarrassing to go home with so little to show for the evening. His mom and dad would be disappointed that he wasn't fitting in . . . again. The almost-empty bag would be proof that he'd been a flop, that he hadn't found a group to hook up with.

"Well, it won't be the first time I've disappointed them," he mumbled, and then an idea came to him.

Taking his wallet from his hip pocket, he found he had seven dollars. He would go to the All-Nite Mini Mart up on Van Buren Street and buy a bunch of candy. Then his parents would never know what a failure he had been.

Already feeling better, Billy cut over to Saratoga Avenue, then made his way through the vacant lot that led to the main thoroughfare through town.

"Hey, it's Billy Boy!" someone called, laughing. "Great costume, Billy. What are you supposed to be—*ugly?*"

Across the vacant lot, headed straight at him through the dark, came a rowdy group of trick-or-treaters, laughing wildly.

"I'm going to suck his bloooood!" said a make-believe Dracula, plastic fangs clicking in his mouth as he walked up with the others.

A girl with her face powdered to a ghastly white and with huge black circles drawn around her eyes giggled. "I'm Dracula's wife," she said. "Who are you supposed to be? A nerd?"

"A nerd it is," said a pirate with a black patch over his eye, a fake hook for a hand, and a cardboard sword in his belt. "Let's see what plunder he has in his bag, maties," he snarled, grabbing at Billy's treat sack.

"Leave me alone!" snapped Billy, pulling his sack away just in the nick of time.

"Better give Long John Silver what he wants," a boy with a fake rubber knife stuck in his head and fake blood all over his face growled. "Better give it to him, or you'll end up like me, with a pain in the brain!"

The group thought this was the funniest thing they'd ever heard, and they were all now in a circle around Billy, laughing and joking. The pirate began poking him with his cardboard sword, and Dracula snarled at him with fake fangs. Billy's palms began to sweat, and he had a sinking feeling inside. He recognized these kids. Brad Kelly was Dracula, Marie Kennedy was Dracula's wife, Pete Cortez was a pirate, and Josh Steinberg was the guy with the rubber knife stuck in his head. They were all the kids he'd asked to go trick-or-treating earlier that day.

"How come you're by yourself, twerp?" Brad Kelly asked, laughing.

Pete Cortez, the pirate, threw an arm around Billy's shoulder. "What's the matter, Billy Boy? Don't you have any friends?"

Pain welled up inside Billy. He *didn't* have a single friend, and he didn't have a good comeback, either. He just looked at his tormentors, then hung his head.

"Answer me!" demanded Pete.

"Come on, guys," said Marie, her chalk-white face actually looking sympathetic. "Quit hassling him."

"Too cheap to buy a mask?" sneered Brad. "Or too stupid?"

"His mommy couldn't think of a costume for her nerdy son," Josh said, adjusting the knife in his head, "so he just went as a geek."

"My mom made a great costume!" Billy practically roared. "You're just too blind to see it!"

"Uh-oh," said Brad sarcastically. "Little Billy's getting mad!"

"What're you supposed to be?" Pete asked snidely as he jabbed Billy with his fake hook.

"Something nobody else thought of," sputtered Billy. "My dad thought of it!"

"What is it he's supposed to have thought of?" asked Pete. "You look like the same stupid kid you always do."

"That's the whole idea," Billy said, trying to control the quaver in his voice. "The idea is to go as a normal human boy."

"How clever!" Josh exclaimed, mocking Billy. "A normal human boy! Now, why didn't I think of that?"

"Because Billy's *daddy* thought of it," Brad said. "Wow, is *he* a genius!"

"Hey," Marie piped in, "I thought you said your mom made you a great costume. Why aren't you wearing it?"

"My mother—" Billy began.

But before he could finish his sentence, Pirate Pete snatched his bag.

"Give that back!" Billy yelled, lunging at him and landing face-first in weeds and dirt. He struggled to his feet. "Give it back, or so help me I'll—!"

"You'll *what?*" scoffed Brad. "Go tell your mommy and daddy?"

"Yeah, I might just do that!" Billy looked at them defiantly. "My parents work for the government, and they could have you terminated."

"*Terminated!*" said Pete, chomping on one of the candy bars from Billy's sack. "As in *killed?*" He laughed so hard he almost choked on the candy bar.

"That's right, killed!" shouted Billy. "So you'd better watch your step with me!"

"Oooooh," said Josh with a snicker. "I'm sooooo scared!" He looked to the others. "Billy's parents work for Uncle Sam, and if we aren't good little boys and girls, he's—"

"Not for Uncle Sam!" Billy shouted. "For Prothos the Great, Inspired Leader of the Planet Zenus!"

"*The Planet Zenus?*" Marie sputtered, then doubled up with laughter.

"Don't you mean *Venus*, idiot?" Brad sneered. "At least use a real planet's name if you're going to make up a lame story."

Billy just glared at him, upset that he had said anything. Marie rolled her eyes. "He really *is* a screwball."

Josh was hardly able to contain himself. "So, Billy. Tell us all about your planet, this planet you and Mom and Pop come from. We'd all be fascinated to learn more."

"You're too stupid to learn anything," Billy snarled. "You're just a bunch of—"

"Oh, so now *we're* stupid, are we?" Brad demanded. He gave Billy a hard push in the chest, then winked at Pete, who quickly got down on all fours behind the terrified boy. Another push, and Billy went sprawling backward over Pete.

"Gee, you okay?" Josh asked, pretending to be sincere as he yanked Billy to his feet and dusted him off. "You were about to enlighten us about Zenus, and about your parents, weren't you?"

"They're scientists!" Billy raged. "They were sent here to see if Earth is worth the trouble of conquering. My parents are the nicest, smartest parents ever! They do everything for me! And my mom *did* make me a costume—the one I wear every day to school, the one I'm wearing right now!" He stopped as if contemplating something. "She made this mask for me, too. It's the mask of a normal human boy. And if you don't believe me, well, I'll just have to show you."

Pete just laughed at him. "You aren't normal, dude. You're—"

But the air went out of his voice. Then his snide expression slowly disappeared and turned to one of horror as Billy whipped off his mask—the mask of a human boy.

Marie screamed.

Brad gasped.

Josh's mouth dropped open like a trapdoor.

They were all stunned as they stared at the human face Billy was holding in his hand . . . then they all gaped at his real face. It was covered with scales, and his reptilian eyes were yellow and glowing. They looked very, *very* angry.

Screams filled the night air as the kids almost fell over each other in their efforts to run away.

* * *

Billy had put his human face back on by the time he returned home. The minute he stepped through the door his parents knew something bad had happened.

"What went wrong, Son?" his dad asked.

"Everything!" Billy cried.

Billy's mom put an arm around him comfortingly. "Calm down and tell us all about it," she said. "It couldn't be that bad."

Billy sat down. "The kids were all so mean. They teased me and pushed me around until I just couldn't take it anymore, until I—"

"Oh, Billy, you didn't!" his mom exclaimed.

"I'm sorry," Billy cried, weeping in earnest now. "I just couldn't help it."

"They know about you?" his dad asked solemnly. "And about us?"

17

Billy nodded.

"Oh, dear," his mother said, wringing her hands. "Now we'll have to get out of town . . . *again*."

"I really made a mess of things," Billy said, lowering his head. "It's all my fault, and I'm—"

Suddenly the sound of a car screeching to a stop interrupted Billy's sentence. He hurried to a window and parted the drapes.

"It's the police!" he cried. "The kids must've told them about me!"

"Calm down," his dad said, walking over to the window and peering out.

"But they're headed up the walk!" Billy cried. "Two of them!"

His dad looked over his shoulder at Billy's mother. "How are we doing as far as animal samples are concerned, dear?"

"We can always use more," she answered. "Especially *human* animals."

There was a heavy knock on the door.

"Well," Billy's dad said, "before we leave town, we might as well ship off a couple more to Zenus."

"Good thinking," Billy's mom said with a smile.

His dad went to the door and opened it. "Good evening, officers," he said. "Is there a problem?"

"We got the strangest call," one of the officers began. "It was about a boy who lives here and, well, he's supposed to be some kind of a monster."

"It's probably just a Halloween prank," the other officer added quickly. "Still, we have to check it out."

"Of course," Billy's dad said pleasantly. "Please come in, officers. By all means, please *do* come in."

*T*he Belmont, which used to be a movie theater, is in a crummy, rundown part of town. Now they put on live shows there with singers, dancers, and comedians. They do cabarets, magic acts, and things like that. Me and my best buddies, Winston and Joey, who are almost fourteen, like me, are standing outside this old dump of a place. It's a Saturday afternoon, and we're bored, just hanging out together, not sure what we want to do, so we decide to give the old Belmont a try. The matinee tickets are only two dollars, and at that price, what've we got to lose? Maybe we'll get a few laughs out of it.

We get our first laugh from the old guy who sells us the tickets. His eyes are all bloodshot, and he's got this big fat red nose that looks all spongy and rotten. He looks like some kind of reject clown.

But it's the guy's false teeth that crack us up the most. They're all loose in his mouth, not attached to anything, and he keeps flipping them around with his tongue and chomping on them as he gives us our change and pushes our tickets toward us.

"Did you see that geek?" Winston asks, laughing so totally out of control that snorting noises are coming out of him.

Me, I'm laughing harder than Winston is, so hard I can't even answer.

And Joey, he's so hysterical it looks like he's going to fall down. I have to practically carry him past the weird-looking ticket taker, who's wearing a white tuxedo that's all grungy with age.

"You boys behave yourself," the tall, sweaty-looking guy says to us as he tears our tickets. "I mean it."

"Yes, sir," Winston says, stifling a snort.

Then we all three salute, click our heels together, and go inside. The smell of stale popcorn mixed with the musty stink of old carpeting and upholstery hits us the minute we walk in.

"Man, this joint's big!" Joey exclaims. "Most of the new theaters are so dinky."

"Yeah," I say, looking around at the few people sitting in the place. "Looks like we can sit just about anywhere we want. This place doesn't look too popular."

We plunk down in three seats near the stage and wait around for a while. The show's supposed to start in a few minutes, but you'd never know it by how dead it is in here. Bored, Joey goes to get us all popcorn, and when he comes back the lights finally dim down. Then a spotlight hits the stage, and this guy comes fumbling out from behind some stained curtains.

"Good afternoon, ladies and gentlemen," he says, his words whistling through his dentures. "Welcome to the Belmont Variety Show! Today, for your entertainment—"

But I'm not even listening to the guy. In fact, I'm about

to bust a gut. The announcer on stage is the same guy with the fake teeth and rotten nose who sold us our tickets!

"Hey," I whisper to my buddies, "this guy's multi-talented. He sells tickets *and* announces the show."

"Yeah," Winston whispers back. "And he probably does all the other acts, too!"

This cracks us up again, and we don't stop until the ratty red curtains crank open, and a guy dressed sort of like a cowboy walks out onstage. He starts telling jokes, and at first they're pretty funny. But then they start getting cornier and cornier.

"Get lost, cowboy!" a guy in the front row calls out. "Go milk a cow!"

That gets a better laugh than any of the comedian's jokes.

"Bring out Sabrina!" yells another guy sitting a few rows in back of us.

The cowboy-comedian shoots a wisecrack at the two hecklers, who quickly scrunch down in their seats as everybody in the place laughs at them. All smiley at his success with the hecklers, the cowboy struts offstage, pretending to be bowlegged, and everybody claps, mainly because he's leaving.

Me, I'm crunching away on some of Joey's thousand-year-old popcorn, actually having an okay time . . . until the next act comes out.

"Oh, no," I groan. "It's the ticket taker. Now he's a tap-dancing accordion player!"

Everybody is practically falling out of their seats, laughing and making fun of the guy as he clatters away in his tap-dancing shoes to the goony music of his accordion. He's got this false smile plastered on his face and he's sweating like crazy. In seconds, his face is all glistening and drippy, and big perspiration stains are running down his shirt.

I actually feel sorry for the guy, but everybody in the place is doubled up laughing. I mean, the guy looks like he just stepped out of a shower! It's unbelievable, but drops of sweat are actually flying off him onto the audience like he's a lawn sprinkler.

"Anybody got an umbrella?" Joey yells.

"We want Sabrina!" two guys call out. Then they start chanting for Sabrina until the soaking-wet, tap-dancing accordion player dances offstage.

For a minute I look around at the audience. It seems like they come just to heckle, laugh, and jeer at the acts. But maybe there's another reason, too. *Who's this Sabrina person they keep yelling for?* I wonder. *Boy, she must really be something.*

Nothing's happening on the stage. It's dead up there. Impatient, everyone starts banging their feet on the floor. It gets louder and louder until finally the sweaty accordion player comes back out, only now he's in the role of master of ceremonies.

He waits for the floor banging to stop, and when it does, he smiles all goofy-like. "And now, what you've all been waiting for," he bellows, beads of sweat still dripping down his face. "Here, for your pleasure, are Sweet Sabrina and Rhonda the Wretched Robot!"

The lights go dim, and right away a change comes over the crowd. Everybody is quiet and respectful. The curtains close. Footsteps can be heard backstage. Then the curtain opens, and seated onstage is a young woman with a ventriloquist's dummy on her lap.

The woman, Sabrina, takes my breath away. With her

auburn hair, flawless skin, and soft brown eyes, she is one of the most beautiful women I have ever seen. She looks about eighteen, or maybe a little bit older, and I can hardly take my eyes off her.

The dummy on her lap is Rhonda, and she's another story. In fact, she's totally hideous. Only about two feet tall, her body is fat and deformed, like a squished marshmallow. Her head is super-awful, too. It's oversized and square-looking, like a robot's. Even from a few rows back, where my friends and I are sitting, I can see that her hair is glued onto her otherwise bald head, and she has phony-looking warts all over her face and hands.

"Hello, everyone," says Sabrina in a sweet, gentle voice. "On behalf of Rhonda and myself, I would like to welcome—"

"Ah, shut up!" Rhonda interrupts in a gruff voice. "The folks ain't here to see you, they're here to see *me*."

"Now, Rhonda, dear," Sabrina coos, "don't be rude. Please don't talk when I'm trying to speak to the nice ladies and gentlemen."

"I got a joke!" Rhonda says, ignoring her. "It's a good one, so shut up!"

I lean forward in my seat as Rhonda tells the joke. But I'm hardly listening. All my focus is on Sabrina. Though her pretty mouth is closed, I can see her lips move, just a tiny bit, as she talks for Rhonda. Her right hand is inside Rhonda's back, and I can tell by the way Sabrina moves now and then that she's manipulating some kind of controls that make Rhonda's mouth open and close, her head turn all jerkylike, and her stubby arms and legs move.

The audience is loving the whole act, hooting with laughter and clapping for more. Rhonda claps for herself, too, slapping her undersized, stumpy-fingered hands together, then throwing an arm around Sabrina's slender neck.

"Thank you, Rhonda," Sabrina says in her gentle, feminine voice. "Now, if it is all right with you, I'd like to sing a song for the audience."

The ugly wooden dummy frowns and swivels its head. Turned almost completely backward, it stares at Sabrina as she begins to sing. There is no music. Only the fragile, crystal-clear sound of Sabrina's glorious voice fills the old theater. It is a special song, a beautiful song. I find it to be as special and beautiful as the person singing it. I am truly mesmerized.

*　*　*

Though the show is long since over, and it is night now, I can still hear Sabrina's song, and I can still see Sabrina singing it. I'm lying on my bed, staring at the ceiling, feeling just wonderful with a vision of Sabrina in my mind, when my dad calls from downstairs, asking me if I want to watch a video he's rented.

"I'm kind of tired," I yell back. "Thanks, anyway."

Now I can go back to thinking about Sabrina, *if* my folks will leave me alone.

"That's not like him *not* to want to see a video," I hear my mom telling my dad. "Maybe he's not feeling well."

"I don't know," my dad says. "He said he's just tired."

In my mind, I see Sabrina stand up. Holding Rhonda, she takes a bow. The curtain closes. Then it opens again, and her whole show starts all over again.

"Sure you don't want to come down?" my dad calls, breaking into my happy thoughts with boring old reality.

"No!" I yell back.

"Let's leave him be," I hear my mom say.

My dad says something back to her, but I don't hear what it is. I don't even try to listen to them anymore. My mind is elsewhere. It's on Sabrina, *totally* on Sabrina.

*   *   *

The next day Winston calls to tell me that we're meeting over at Sanderson Park to play baseball, which is what we do almost every Sunday. I tell him I'm sick and can't play.

"Well, hope ya feel better," he says. "Later."

Then I go and tell my folks I'm going to play baseball, only I really head to town, to the Belmont to see the Sunday matinee. To see Sabrina.

I realize I'm sort of like falling in love. I go and see both the Saturday and Sunday matinees every weekend now. I even go to the Friday night shows when I can sneak out. Sometimes I go with my buddies, but mostly I go alone. I don't like to share Sabrina with anybody.

I know her act backward and forward. I know all of her songs by heart. I know all the jokes Rhonda tells, all the weird stuff she says, and even every one of her jerky little movements.

I guess you could say I'm becoming a real expert on the show. In fact, I've started noticing little things. For example, Sabrina always wears very pretty, sort of old-fashioned dresses in long prints with high necks and a touch of lace. Usually she sits with her legs crossed at the ankles, and everything about her is very proper and ladylike, and she always smiles sweetly. Most of the time, her left hand is in her lap while her right hand is inside the dummy's back, working the controls.

Rhonda is the absolute opposite. She's noisy, rude, and jerks around like a robot. The frown on her face never goes away. A lot of the time, she stares at Sabrina and always fiddles and plays with the fake warts on her hands.

Obviously a big part of the act is the contrast between Sabrina and the dummy. One's so beautiful and the other's so awful. That's why the act goes over so well. Still, sometimes as I sit watching the show I wonder if Sabrina wouldn't be better off working with a better-looking dummy. It bothers me to see her with such a horrible creature, even if Rhonda isn't real.

It also bothers me that Sabrina works in a dump like the Belmont Theater. She deserves better. My friends all think I'm crazy, falling for Sabrina the way I have. They act like I've abandoned them, and they tell me I'm nuts for spending all my time at the Belmont and for not being out doing "fun" stuff like sports and goofing off at the mall.

"Man, how could you fall for a stupid ventriloquist?" Joey keeps ragging on me all the time. "Even if she *is* beautiful, she works in such a geeky place."

"She's too old for you anyway, man," says Winston. "And *too* pretty. Why would she want to have anything to do with a kid?"

I don't really have an answer. I know I'm too young, and Sabrina would never want to be my girlfriend or anything like that. I'm not *completely* unrealistic about the situation.

But I also know something else about Sabrina. She's sweet and nice and would never do anything to hurt anybody's feelings. Mine included. I can tell by the way she looks at me during her show. It's a look that I carry with me wherever I go, a look I want to see close up. And now I know that what I thought when I first saw her is true. I know I just *have* to meet Sabrina. And the time to do it is coming *very* soon.

* * *

Today is Friday, and I've decided that tonight is when it's going to happen. In fact, I've been thinking about it all through my classes and all through lunch. Finally, when the last bell rings, I race home and start laying the groundwork for my parents. I make up some story about how Joey and I are sleeping over at Winston's house. They always let me go over to his house because he's a straight-A student and they think it'll rub off on me.

Anyway, I clue in Winston to intercept my calls for me in case my parents check up on things. Then I head downtown to the Belmont to see Sabrina.

I'm nervous as I watch the show, nervous that my folks will find out that I lied to them, nervous that they'll some-how squeeze the truth out of Winston and come to get me. In some ways I wish they would, because what really has me shaking is what I plan to do as soon as the show's over. I'm going to try to get backstage and actually meet Sabrina, maybe get her autograph, and even talk to her a little.

Before I know it, the show ends, the houselights go on, and the announcer with the mouthful of false teeth goes through the "thank-you-for-coming" routine. The people file out. But not me. I scoot off into the shadows, then up the stairs, half-hidden behind the folds of the huge red curtain.

Bare bulbs light the way along a creepy corridor, and turning a corner, I see a bunch of dressing room doors. A second later I'm standing in front of one with a cockeyed paper star tacked to it. The name SABRINA is written in black marker on the star.

"What're you doin' back here?" somebody demands from behind me.

I turn around and stare right into the face of the sweating ticket taker, master of ceremonies, tap-dancing accordion player. He's wearing a soaking-wet undershirt and tuxedo pants with the suspenders dragging on the floor.

"I came to get Sabrina's autograph," I say, expecting to be tossed out on my ear.

Instead the guy's lips peel back over his yellow teeth in an amused grin, and he hammers on the door with his meaty fist. "Hey, ya got an admirer!" he calls.

"Who is it?" I hear Sabrina ask from inside in her sweet, feminine voice.

"Some kid." There's a long pause.

"Send the brat in!" Rhonda cackles.

"Yes, do come in," Sabrina says softly.

"Go for it, kid," the sweaty man tells me, pushing open the door and gesturing me inside with his thumb. "Yer sweet on her, ain't ya?" He winks. "Don't blame ya. She's a real looker!"

The dressing room is large and dark, lit only by the neon green of the BELMONT THEATER marquee outside the window. Across the room, on a shabby sofa beneath the window, sits Sabrina, gazing sweetly at me. Her right hand, as always, is in the back of Rhonda, who's sitting beside her, frowning like she usually does and playing with the warts on her hands.

"Hi," I say, my voice sounding weird and off-key. I rock from foot to foot. "I-I'm kind of nervous," I blurt out, wondering why I said it.

"What's your name?" Sabrina asks in the kindest voice I've ever heard.

I tell her my name, and for some stupid reason I give her my age, too. Boy, what a nerd I can be sometimes!

Rhonda laughs. "So, you think Sabrina's pretty? You like her, huh?"

"Yes," I admit to her, then turn my gaze bashfully back toward Sabrina. "I've seen all your shows. Maybe you think I'm just a stupid kid, but I think you're great, and you're so pretty that—"

"Yeah," Rhonda sneers, "you *are* a stupid kid."

My face gets all red.

Sabrina smiles from across the room. "Well," she says, "*I* think you're very nice." She blinks. "And it was nice of you to come to see my act, and to come see me here."

My face gets even redder.

Rhonda punches Sabrina in the side. "Ya think he's so cute, Sabrina, why don't you give the boy a big kisserooni!"

Sabrina flips on a light, and then to my astonishment, she gets up and is walking toward me! I'm petrified. Is she actually going to give me a kiss?

"Look at the lovesick kid!" Rhonda cackles.

Sabrina keeps walking toward me, and I edge away, closer to the ugly dummy, who's still sitting on the shabby couch.

"What's wrong, lover boy?" Rhonda chortles, her squarish head cocked to one side as she kicks her under-sized legs against the side of the sofa.

Now, *that* gets my eyes off Sabrina. I stare at Rhonda, and at first I don't get it. Then I don't *want* to get it. I don't want to believe what I'm seeing. How can *Rhonda* be kicking her legs? How can *she* be talking? How can *her* lips be moving? How, if Sabrina isn't beside her, working the controls, can *Rhonda* do anything?

Sabrina turns in my direction and continues toward me, smiling.

"How do ya like the girl of your dreams?" Rhonda sneers.

I'm looking at the backs of Rhonda's hands, at what I thought were warts. But now I can see that they're not warts at all. They're buttons!

She jabs one . . . and Sabrina stops.

"Understand how the act works now?" Rhonda demands. "Ya starting to get the idea, kid?" She pushes another warty button.

"Hello, everyone," Sabrina says. "On behalf of Rhonda and myself, I would like to welcome you to our show."

I walk over and touch Sabrina's face, her perfect, beautiful face. It feels synthetic . . . and ice cold.

Out in the hall I hear laughter.

Rhonda taps a control button. From inside Sabrina comes the squeal of a rewinding tape.

"No!" I cry.

"Hello, everyone," says Sabrina. "On behalf of Rhonda and myself, I would like to welcome you to our show."

I am crying as I rush out the door. I run down the corridor, laughter burning in my ears. The cowboy-comedian and the denture-wearing ticket seller, master of ceremonies, and sweating, tap-dancing accordion player, they're watching me go . . . and they sound like they're having the laugh of their lives.

30

THE THIRTEENTH FLOOR

*F*ifteen-year-old Norman Wermeir was terrified and miserable wearing his stupid baggy suit, wedged between his mom and his little sister in the backseat of the taxi as it plowed through traffic. In the front seat, next to the driver, was his father.

"We're going to have a great time," said his dad, looking back over the seat.

Norman said nothing. He *knew* how wrong his dad was, that something bad, something *horrible*, was going to happen. It was Friday the 13th. And the cab was driving up 13th street in the city of Boston in Massachusetts, one of the original thirteen states admitted to the Union. He looked at his watch and saw that it was almost one o'clock, which in military time was 1300 hours.

Thirteen! The number felt as though it were burning a hole in Norman's brain. He took out his rabbit's foot from his pocket and began to rub it.

"Norman's starting up with his freaky superstitious

stuff again," chortled his younger sister, Paula, noticing the rabbit's foot. "That's so *stupid*."

"It's not stupid," Norman snapped. "Don't any of you see what's happening? We're headed right into something weird, something evil. Why can't any of you realize that?"

His dad turned around and looked back at him. "Norman, you've got to get over this"—he fumbled for words— "this *hang-up* of yours. Especially all this stuff about the number thirteen. We've been planning this trip for a long time. And not only are you ruining it for yourself, you're ruining it for all of us. So let's have a good time, okay, pal?"

Norman slouched in the seat and said nothing. *What's the purpose of arguing?* he thought darkly. *They'll never understand.*

"How much farther to the hotel?" his dad asked the driver.

"It's just up ahead, sir," the man replied.

A silence settled over the cab as it continued on—for thirteen more blocks. In his head, Norman ticked them off, one by one.

Finally the driver pulled up in front of the Wilmont Regency, and instantly a strange feeling swept through Norman. Then, as they walked into the lobby, the feeling grew even stronger.

"I've been here before," he said.

"What are you talking about, Norman?" his dad asked. "You've never even been to *Boston* before."

Norman looked around. "But everything seems so familiar."

Paula rolled her eyes. "You are definitely a weird brother!"

"Please, Norman," his mother begged. "Don't start anything."

"I'm getting really tired of all this strange talk of yours," his dad said sternly. "Now, give it a rest, will you?" With a look of annoyance on his face, he headed over to the registration desk, where a very tall woman with large dark eyes was waiting to greet him.

Sulking angrily, Norman wandered around the lobby while his mom and sister followed his dad. He was *positive* he had been in the hotel before. The pink-and-green floral carpeting, the new-looking rose-colored sofas, the ornate crystal chandeliers, he was *sure* he'd seen them all before . . . but when?

Suddenly Norman heard a strange whirring noise. Turning, he saw that it was coming from the hotel elevator. A fancy replica of an earlier model, the elevator was *definitely* something he'd seen before.

Norman walked over to the old contraption. Through the cage-like grillwork of the thing he looked down into the shaft. It was a dark, rectangular hole with thick electric cables hanging down into it. As he looked, Norman could see the head of a man at floor level followed by the rest of him. Then the guy was standing there, inside the elevator, inside a cage within a cage, looking out at Norman.

"Going up?" the man, obviously the elevator operator, asked as he rattled open the gilded gatelike door. The interior of the elevator had plush green carpeting and mirrored walls.

"No," Norman said, backing away. He stared at the operator, a short man with red hair and a large mole on his cheek.

"Something wrong?" the man asked.

Norman realized he was staring but still couldn't take his eyes off the guy. He'd seen him somewhere. But where?

"Uh, I didn't push the button," Norman said, embarrassed. "I—I didn't call for an elevator."

The odd little man shrugged but said nothing as Norman quickly retreated to where his parents and Paula were standing next to a bellboy who had all their luggage piled high on a cart. At first Norman thought the bellboy was a kid, but then he realized he was just a very small man with an oversized head.

"Mom," Norman whispered, taking his mother aside. "I don't want to stay in this place. It gives me the creeps."

"It's a beautiful hotel!" she exclaimed, looking around.

His father came up behind them. "*Now* what's wrong?"

"It's hard to explain," Norman began, "but something is wrong."

"*What?*" his father demanded impatiently.

"I don't know, but something is going to happen, something really strange."

Paula laughed. "*You're* really strange!"

"Nothing is going to happen," said his dad. "Now, please, Norman, try to get a grip on yourself."

Norman was about to say something when he felt his mother put a hand on his shoulder. "Relax," she said, trying to calm him down. "Try to put all these silly thoughts out of your head. Will you do that for me?" And with that she followed the bellman who was going to show them to their rooms.

"Nobody ever listens to me," Norman muttered, trailing along behind his family toward the elevator.

"What floor?" the operator asked, sounding a little bored.

"Room 1302," Norman's dad said, glancing at the number on the key in his hand.

"Oh, good!" Paula exclaimed, throwing an evil wink at her brother. "The thirteenth floor!"

"That does it!" Norman snapped, storming out of the elevator. "I'm not staying in this hotel! Not on the thirteenth floor!"

"You get back in this elevator," his mother demanded.

"No way!" Norman shouted, his hands defiantly on his hips.

Asking the operator to wait for him, Norman's dad made his way out of the elevator to where Norman was standing. "Be reasonable, Norman," he said. "Stop all this foolishness."

"It's *not* foolishness," Norman insisted.

For a moment his dad was at a loss for words. Then he pointed at one of the rose-colored sofas. "We're going up to the room," he said. "And you, young man, are going to sit on that sofa until you come to your senses."

Norman just stood there. "I'm not a little kid you can order around!" he snapped.

"You *are* a kid," his father said sternly. "And you're acting like a baby."

"No, I'm not. I'm growing up, in case you haven't noticed."

"Not fast enough." Livid, his dad stormed back into the elevator. "Take 'er up," he told the operator. Then he glowered at Norman. "I expect to see you upstairs in a few moments."

"Well, I hope I never see you again!" Norman yelled at his family inside the old cage of an elevator. "Any of you!"

"You should be careful of what you hope for," the operator warned him as he pulled a lever. "You just might get it."

"Well, I hope I do!" Norman shouted, feeling a little silly for overreacting but unable to retract his words without feeling even sillier.

The fancy grillwork door clattered shut. There was a hum, and Norman watched as his family disappeared upward in the elevator.

*　*　*

For a long while Norman stood in the lobby, his anger increasing with each passing minute. Finally, unable to endure it any longer, he stormed out of the hotel, his jaw clenched with fury.

Alone, he prowled the streets of the unfamiliar city. He sat on a bench in a park full of statues, then trudged down a bike path, and finally wandered through a graveyard. He felt so rotten, lonely, and unwanted, as though he were an outcast from his own family.

Pouting, he thought about how mad he was at his parents, at stupid Paula, and, he had to admit, at himself. A lot of the bickering and fighting, he knew deep down, was his own fault. He had, as his folks had said, "changed, and gotten moody and obsessed with dark, morbid ideas lately." But he couldn't help it. How could he explain to his parents that some strange, evil force seemed to gradually be taking over his life?

He'd never been superstitious before, but now he was afraid of black cats, walking under ladders, and especially of the number thirteen. He knew, somewhere deep inside, that it was all irrational. Yet even now as he walked along the sidewalk, he watched to make sure he didn't step on any cracks.

Norman knew that eventually he'd have to return to the hotel, and so he started heading in that direction. But he wasn't ready to go back, not yet. Not only was he genuinely afraid of the place, he was still angry and upset. He had to save *some* face. It was only two-thirty, after all, and heading back so soon would be, well, embarrassing.

But what could he do? How could he kill some time without being bored to death? Then he noticed the movie theater just up the street from the hotel, so he hurried over, bought a ticket, and went inside.

The title of the movie, *Collision Course*, had sounded like it would have lots of good action, but it turned out to be a boring drama about a man and a woman fighting to get control of a farm. The weird thing about it was that as the movie went on, Norman realized he'd seen it before— long ago, but he had no recollection of where or when. Bored with the movie, and tired from the trip, he drifted off to sleep.

* * *

It was dark when Norman came out of the theater. Groggy, miserable, and wondering what his parents would say when he showed up, Norman headed down the street toward the hotel. His eyes were blurry, his bones and joints felt achy and stiff, and the chill wind of the night air blasted right through the stupid old suit his parents had made him wear on the plane. For some reason the suit felt tight, and so did his collar.

That's odd, he thought. *These clothes used to be big on me.*

He was shivering as he hurried into the hotel. He hadn't noticed anything different about the place from outside. But once he was in the lobby, he was startled to see how the place had changed. Everything seemed older and the whole place smelled musty, sort of like a tomb.

For a moment Norman thought he was in the wrong hotel, but then he saw a faded gold-and-brown placard on the wall above the registration desk: WILMONT REGENCY, it read.

He looked around. The pink-and-green floral carpeting was definitely the same, except now it was faded and threadbare. The rose-colored sofas, which before had looked practically brand-new, now looked lumpy and frayed, and the large crystal chandelier in the center of the lobby, though lit brightly, was so dusty the light hardly shined through.

Suddenly Norman heard a groaning, whirring noise. He turned and saw it was coming from the hotel elevator. He started to race toward it, eager to go up and find his family, but he had to slow down. For some reason his pants had become so small that he was afraid he'd split them.

The elevator arrived, and Norman passed through the grimy, age-worn grillwork.

"Going up?" the operator asked, his voice a dead monotone.

Norman wanted to scream. The operator was the same one as before, only now he was old and wrinkled, his red hair considerably thinner, and the dark mole on his cheek was much larger.

The man smiled, revealing long yellow teeth. "Something wrong?"

Norman just stared at him, unable to answer.

"What floor?" the old man asked.

"Th-thirteenth," Norman finally managed to stammer.

The operator gave Norman an odd, knowing look. "There *is* no thirteenth floor," he said.

"Huh?" Norman looked puzzled. "What do you mean?"

"There's no thirteenth floor," the man repeated, not changing a single inflection in his chilling voice.

Norman did a double take. "What's going on here?" he asked, a feeling of horror crawling up his spine. "Is this some kind of weird joke or something?"

"You going up or not?" the old man asked, a blank expression on his face.

Norman backed away, then hurried to the registration desk. He had to bang on the metal handbell several times before a woman came out from a back room. She was the same very tall woman with large dark eyes as before, but now she was old and stoop-shouldered.

"May I help you?" she asked in a pinched-sounding voice.

Norman told her what the elevator operator had said about there not being any thirteenth floor.

The woman nodded. "That is correct. The Wilmont Regency used to have a thirteenth floor, but people became superstitious after the fire. And so it was eliminated."

"Wh-what fire?" Norman stammered.

"Years ago we had a fire, on the thirteenth floor. Oh, it was dreadful! After the repairs, the numbers were changed." The woman shrugged. "It's just silly superstition, but now the numbers go 11 . . . 12 . . .*14*, instead of 11 . . . 12 . . . *13*. So I guess you could say, sir, that the fourteenth floor, the top floor, is actually the thirteenth floor."

"In the fire," Norman asked, wondering why the woman had called him *sir*, "was anybody hurt?"

The woman looked uncomfortable. "Yes, and three people died." She paused for a moment. "But that was a long—"

"*Died!*" Norman almost screamed. "My parents were on that floor!"

"I don't understand, sir," said the woman. "I'm sorry if—"

But Norman wasn't listening. Baffled, on the verge of panic, he hurried back to the elevator. "Where is my family?" he demanded of the old operator.

The man inside the cage smiled oddly.

"You know something, don't you?" Norman accused him.

The old man nodded.

"What did you do with my family?"

"It wasn't *my* doing," the old man said calmly. "It was *yours*."

"What do you mean, *mine*?" Norman asked, his voice raspy and quavering.

"I warned you before," the old man said. "You should be careful of what you wish for."

"Well, what I *wish* for now is to go to room 1302!"

"You mean 1402, sir," the operator corrected him.

"Just take me up!" Norman ordered.

"As you wish, sir."

"And quit calling me sir!" Norman barked, getting into the elevator. And then he saw his reflection in the mirrored walls.

He was a middle-aged man!

The operator rattled the gate closed, then pulled a lever, sending the elevator squealing upward. Sweating and having trouble catching his breath, Norman stared at his multiple reflections in the scratched mirrors on the walls. He turned his attention to the floor indicator. Eyes wide, he watched as the numbers lit up: 9 . . . 10 . . . 11 . . . 12 . . . 14!

The elevator bounced slightly as it came to a stop. "Your floor, sir," the operator said, breaking into a crooked smile.

Norman stepped into the hallway of the seedy old hotel. Everything looked dingy, and there was evidence of repair work and repainting done long ago. He hurried to the room with the number 1402 on the door and pounded on it.

The door opened a crack, and a grumpy-looking woman peered out. "Yeah? Who are you?" she asked gruffly.

"I'm looking for my parents," Norman said urgently. "And for my sister, Paula. They were all in this room, but that was a long time ago, and now I can't find them anywhere."

"Ah, go away. You're nuts," the woman grumbled, slamming the door in Norman's face.

He ran back to the elevator. "What happened to my family?" he begged the old man.

"Lost in the fire," the operator answered, grinning evilly.

"And me, what happened to *me*? I was young, but now I'm—"

"You grew up," the old man sneered. "At least now people won't treat you like a little kid anymore."

"But I *am* a little kid," Norman insisted. "Or at least I was."

The old man shrugged. "Now you have everything you asked for!" And with that he laughed darkly and pulled a lever.

Staring in horror, Norman watched as the elevator started its descent. Inside, the pasty-faced old operator began to disappear from view, his terrible laughter following him down the shaft as he vanished from sight.

Norman took a few faltering steps backward. "Mom! Dad!" he screamed again and again, alone in the hallway of what had once been the Wilmont Regency's thirteenth floor.

Up and down the hall a few doors opened. People looked out, annoyed and puzzled at the middle-aged man standing in the middle of the hallway, crying for his parents . . . like a little boy.

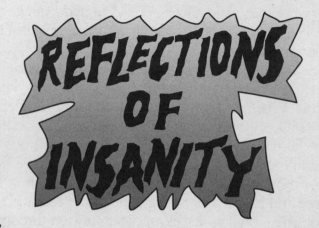

REFLECTIONS OF INSANITY

*L*ightning crackled across the black night sky in ugly zigzag patterns that looked like giant electrical spiders. Thunder rumbled and seemed to split open the universe. Rain poured down in great drifting sheets.

Carol Jane Ellery, fifteen, hurried up the walkway to her house, holding a newspaper over her head and splashing through puddles in her already sopping-wet shoes. Above the front door a narrow metal overhang seemed almost alive with the tinny sound of rain drumming down on it. Huddling under the overhang to get away from the cold and wet, Carol fumbled under the mat for an extra key.

"Darn it!" she grumbled when she found nothing there. She looked under the potted plant and felt with her dripping fingers along the ledge above the doorjamb, again with no luck.

Once more braving the torrential rain, she hurried around to the back of the house. Even before trying the knob on the back door, she knew it was hopeless, and she knew what she would have to do. *Mom and Dad are going to be mad,* she told herself. *But I'll die of pneumonia if I stay out here any longer.*

Resolved to her task, she pulled off a shoe and, grimacing, whacked the heel of it against a kitchen window. When nothing happened, she hit it harder. The glass suddenly crunched and shattered inward, scattering razor-sharp pieces all over a kitchen counter inside.

Startled, worried that the neighbors may have heard, Carol carefully reached through the large jagged hole she'd created and brushed as much glass off the counter as she could. Then, pulling herself up, she crawled through the window. She was just lowering herself from the countertop into the kitchen when suddenly a shard of glass gashed her wrist, and almost in the same instant, a sharp piece on the floor stabbed right through her thinly soled shoe.

By the time she finally made her way across the kitchen to flip on the light, she was in real pain and bleeding a lot. In fact, a trail of blood led from the broken window across the kitchen floor, and there were bloody smears on the wall around the light switch. It practically looked like a murder scene.

"Oh, great!" she groaned as she washed blood from her hands in the kitchen sink. "This is all I need! Mom and Dad will kill me now."

Pulling half a dozen paper towels from the roller under the cupboard, she wiped the blood from her leg and wrist. She made a halfhearted attempt to clean up the mess on the kitchen floor, then hurried to the guest bathroom, where she left red smears on a turquoise bath towel. She was glad to see that though the cuts had bled a lot at first, they actually were quite small, and she quickly bandaged them.

Feeling better, Carol made her way into the hall. To her surprise there was a light on at the top of the stairs. *Could they be home?* she wondered. *Surely they would have heard me breaking in.*

"Anybody home?" Carol called out. "Mom? Dad? Are you up there?"

When only silence greeted her, Carol decided that her parents must have left the light on by accident when they left for work that morning. She glanced at the luminous dial on her oversized wristwatch. It was almost six-thirty. *Where in the world are they?* she wondered. *They're usually home by now.*

Being alone in the house was definitely *not* what Carol needed right now. Earlier that day news had come over the radio that there had been an escape from Ginsberg Mental Health Facility, less than three miles from town, *her* town, Hampton Falls, Vermont. The escapee was an insane murderess who had brutally slain an elderly couple and their grandson.

Carol had read all about it that morning. According to the newspaper, the murderess, after being found legally insane and incompetent to stand trial, had been committed to the Ginsberg Facility over the protests of the residents of Hampton Falls. They were terrified that she would escape and kill again. Now the reassurance from the police and the director of the hospital that the murderess could *never* escape the maximum-security unit had suddenly proved to be nothing more than empty words.

The paper reported that, after knocking a hospital

orderly unconscious, the woman had escaped the institution by concealing herself in the backseat of a doctor's car. Once on the highway, brandishing a spoon she'd sharpened into a point, she robbed the man of his jewelry and other items, then ordered him to drive down a narrow dirt road. Then, after suddenly telling him to stop, she jumped out of the car and fled into the woods on foot.

Whether the murderess was still in the woods or was on the loose somewhere in Hampton Falls had not been determined. Regardless, everyone in town, including Carol, was scared to death. Police had warned residents to stay inside, keep their doors locked, and keep a watch out for the murderess or for anything suspicious.

After turning up the thermostat and shedding her sopping-wet coat, Carol made her way into the den. Flipping on the light, she noticed something different about the room. The furniture was the same but some of it had been moved. *Guess Mom got into one of her moods to do some rearranging,* Carol decided, finding the television remote and turning the set on.

She was just in time to catch the end of a segment about the escaped murderess on the six o'clock news. A familiar face flashed on the screen. Carol sat down and watched as a reporter interviewed the mother of the young boy who had been slain.

"Ronnie was such a happy little kid," the thin red-haired lady said. "So full of life and energy, and so smart. He was only nine years old, but he could beat just about anybody at chess. Who knows? He might have grown up to be a champion." The woman brushed away a tear. "Now he'll never grow up at all."

The picture on the screen changed to a close-up of a

chess set as the woman picked up the king and held it lovingly, her head hanging.

"How sad," Carol muttered to herself. "That poor woman. That poor little boy." She blinked back the tears in her own eyes. "Who could do such a thing?"

Not wanting to see more of the woman's grief, Carol changed the channel, only to find another telecast about the same story. The anchorwoman, an Asian lady with long dark hair, was interviewing a psychiatrist.

"In layman's terms, Dr. Garrison," she asked, "what is the nature of the murderess's disorder?"

The psychiatrist, a pudgy, balding man, appeared nervous. "Well," he said, clearing his throat, "the individual with this disorder has great difficulty distinguishing the real from the unreal. Simply speaking, such a person does not know who he or she is, and would have little or no memory of committing a crime, even one such as murder. Other symptoms include confusion, disorientation, and auditory and visual hallucinations. For example, the individual might see things that aren't there and hear voices in his or her head."

"What is the cause of this disorder?" the anchorwoman asked.

"Often it can be traced to a chemical imbalance in the brain, and recently a number of medications have been developed which are generally quite successful in treating the illness. In this case, however, the treatment—"

But Carol didn't wait for him to finish. "I don't need to scare myself any more than I already am," she declared. Then she pushed the OFF button on the remote, and the screen went dark.

Trying to shake the horrid story from her mind, Carol

went to a front window and, parting a curtain, peered out. The rain, at long last, had stopped. The wind, though, continued to gust, blowing little showers of water off the leaves of trees. Now and then a car crept by, its tires hissing down the wet street.

Around a corner a police car came into view. It was moving slowly, the beam of its searchlight probing the blackness, flashing across the fronts of houses, briefly lighting up fences, trees, and cars. For a moment the beam came to rest on Carol's house, then the car eased away. It sped up and soon became nothing more than twin red taillights shrinking into the night.

Carefully putting the curtains back into place, Carol made her way into the kitchen. A cool wind whipped through the shattered window, and bits of broken glass sparkled on the countertop and floor. On the walls and window frame were red-brown fingerprints of drying blood.

Carol examined the bandages on her wrist and leg. They were staying on nicely, and her cuts had stopped bleeding and hardly hurt at all. But what a mess her cuts and the broken window had left!

Hungry, she poked around in the refrigerator and found some cold cuts, fruit salad, and cottage cheese. She made a plate for herself and sat down at the table to eat, wondering where her parents could possibly be.

Suddenly the phone on the wall behind her rang. She jumped out of her seat, startled. Had her parents been in an accident? Is that why they were late? Her flesh crawled with fear as she picked up the receiver.

"Hello," she answered haltingly.

For a moment she heard a static-laced voice—a woman's voice. Then there was silence.

"Who is this?" Carol asked, her voice weak and faltering.

Again there was silence, and then raspy breathing. Was it her mother? Was she hurt?

"Hello!" Carol demanded.

There was a click on the other end of the line. Momentarily the connection went dead, followed by a dial tone.

Carol hung up. *Lines must be down, or messed up by the storm*, she reasoned. But she only half-believed it. Someone, perhaps the escaped murderess, was playing games with her, tormenting her. Suddenly her appetite vanished, and Carol felt a wave of nausea run through her. She also felt the beginning of a headache. Covering her half-eaten meal with plastic wrap, she put it back in the refrigerator.

She was just rinsing off the silverware when suddenly she went rigid with fear. Somewhere in the house, perhaps upstairs, a door slammed shut.

The wind is still gusting and someone probably left a window open, she told herself. For a moment her whole body relaxed until her imagination took over. Or is there another, far more frightening explanation? Is there someone upstairs?

Tense, her nerves on edge, Carol made her way from the kitchen into the hallway. Floorboards creaked overhead, and another door shut upstairs, this time more softly.

Terrified, Carol hurried to a phone. She picked it up and was already dialing 911 when she realized the line was dead.

Run! Get out of the house! a voice in her head yelled.

Relax, said another, more rational voice. *You're getting all worked up over nothing.*

But try as she might, she could not rid herself of her fears. Why hadn't the extra key been in one of the usual hiding places? Had someone—the killer—found the key and let herself in? Had the murderess turned on the light upstairs? Was she somewhere in the house? Hiding in another room . . . in a closet . . . under a bed?

Get a grip! she told herself. *You're letting your imagination run away with you!*

Taking a deep breath, Carol made her way up the stairs, one step at a time. Reaching the second-floor landing, she saw light coming from a partially open door. And then her hair stood on end. From inside the room she heard footsteps. Then there was a click as another, brighter light went on, and almost in the same instant a TV began to blare.

Terrified, Carol pressed her back against a wall, her heart pounding in her chest. *Who's in that room?* A voice in her head screamed. *Who?*

She crept toward the top of the stairs, ready to flee down them when suddenly she heard a voice coming from inside the room. Dread welled up within her. It was a woman's voice!

Carol stood rooted to the spot, too terrified to move. Her breath came in hissing gasps.

Suddenly she heard another voice. It was her father's!

"Don't hurt anybody," he said. "And we don't want you to get hurt, either."

Then came her mother's voice. "Please try to understand that everybody only wants to help you," she said. "You've got to believe that!"

The insane killer has Mom and Dad! Carol's mind exploded with fear. *I've got to help them!*

Pushing open the door a crack more, Carol gazed in. She was ready to hurl herself at the killer, but instead she found herself gaping in disbelief and confusion at the TV. There on the screen, she saw her parents sitting together on a sofa in their house being interviewed. But it wasn't the house she remembered growing up in. And her parents looked different, too. Somehow they looked a lot older.

"As I understand it," the newscaster interviewing Carol's parents was saying, "you moved from your home in Hampton Falls here to Timberlaine shortly after the murders. Is that right?"

"Yes," Carol's father said. "We sold the house lock, stock, and barrel—completely furnished."

"It was no longer home to us," her mother explained. "With all the memories, it was just too painful to take anything with us."

What are they talking about? Carol asked herself. *Why are they lying, saying they sold our house? I'm standing right in it.*

The newscaster stood alone on the screen. "As you have just heard, from their home here in Timberlaine, the parents of the troubled young lady who escaped today are very worried about her. They believe she is wandering in a state of confusion, probably not even knowing where she is or even *who* she is."

Carol watched in awe as the scene switched to a final shot of her parents.

"If you are where you can see this broadcast, honey," her mother said, "please just remember how much we love you."

Then came her dad's final comment. "Go to the authorities, to the police, or the hospital. They'll help you, sweetheart."

Why are my parents on TV? wondered Carol. *Why would they be making such bizarre statements?*

Suddenly remembering that the killer was probably watching television in the room right before her, Carol pushed open the door. As it opened wider, a teenage girl came into view. She was slouched on a sofa, wearing headphones connected to a CD player and bobbing her head to the music as she thumbed through a magazine. She was totally oblivious of the blaring TV and of Carol, who was creeping up behind her.

Suddenly Carol stopped. *What's going on?* a voice shrieked inside her head. She quickly began backing out of the room. *Why is that girl in my house? Could she be the murderess?*

Gradually Carol became aware of soft crying coming from the room at the end of the hall, coming from *her* own bedroom. Slowly, very quietly, she made her way down the hall and into the bedroom. Standing there in total surprise, she realized it had been turned into a nursery. In the crib a toddler, a cute little girl, was whining, as though she were just waking up from a nap.

"Poor, sweet little cutie-pie," Carol murmured as she began to make her way toward the crib.

And then suddenly she wanted to scream in horror.

Coming toward her was a young woman, the girl whose face she had seen in the newspaper, the insane murderess, wearing a man's overcoat, her hair hanging damp against her face, her eyes wide with fear.

Frantically Carol searched for something with which to

defend herself. There was nothing; but then she reached into the pocket of her coat and took out what looked like a spoon that had been sharpened into a point.

The toddler sat up in her crib. Her sniveling turned into screechy, anguished bawling.

"Quiet!" Carol hissed. She didn't want the little girl to draw the attention of the killer creeping closer. The sharpened spoon raised above her head, Carol rushed at the girl. "Quiet!" she demanded again, clamping a hand over the child's mouth.

"Quiet!" the murderess hissed, mimicking Carol. She also had a sharpened spoon raised above her head.

"Leave us alone!" Carol screamed. Then taking her hand from the child's mouth, she approached the killer fearfully.

"Leave us alone!" the murderess parroted, her spoon still raised, ready to attack.

"Get back! I'm warning you!" Carol snarled, continuing to stalk the murderess—as the murderess stalked her. "You're not going to touch that child!" she screamed, planting herself between the killer and the little girl.

Then, shrieking insanely, Carol lunged at the killer, repeatedly slashing and stabbing at her own reflection in the mirror before her.

MR. X

I have a nervous, sick feeling as I head across campus from the boys' gym to my English class, my last class of the day. Ms. Soto is going to announce the winner of the writing contest she holds every month. This month we all had to write a nonfiction narrative, and I think mine is good enough to win.

As I walk into class and take my seat I try not to get my hopes up too high. I've never won the writing contest before, and I guess I shouldn't expect things to be different today. Still, I think my story, one I call "Mr. X," is the best I've ever written. I put an awful lot into it, and who knows, maybe I do have a shot at winning.

The bell rings, and everybody is sort of clowning around until Ms. Soto stands up at her desk and says, "Okay, people. Settle down." After a little more chair-squeaking and jabbering, the class gets quiet, and for a moment, almost too quiet. Like me, everyone is waiting for the announcement of the contest winner.

Finally Ms. Soto starts taking attendance. I'm watching her and thinking how I wish she weren't married. I've had a crush on her ever since I laid eyes on her. She's pretty and real smart, not like any of the dumb girls in my school.

But Ms. Soto is also real tough. You can't get away with much with her. I mean, it's not like any of us are scared of her. It's more that we all like her and respect her. She's one of those teachers, those rare ones, that you think of as a friend and whose opinion actually matters.

The stack of stories is sitting right on her desk. Mine is in there. And I get all nervous again. Boy, do I want to win.

The suspense is really getting to me, and I start to feel like slimy worms are crawling around in my stomach. I try not to think about it and put my head on my desk.

Suddenly Ms. Soto stops taking attendance. "Are you feeling all right, Andy?" I hear her ask, and shock waves of embarrassment hit me.

"I'm fine, Ms. Soto," I mutter, raising my head.

"Then please sit up and join the class, won't you?"

Ted Rosenbloom looks over his shoulder and gives me a you're-a-nerd look. Denise Thompson giggles at me. Jack Lewis, who's just about my best friend in Ms. Soto's class, tells Denise to shut up.

"Quiet, please, over there!" Ms. Soto snaps. "Unless you'd all like to wait until tomorrow to find out who won this month's contest."

This shuts everyone up, and Ms. Soto picks up the stack of stories. She starts walking around the room, handing them back.

I watch, holding my breath. She passes by my desk twice *without* handing my paper back. That means she might read mine out loud. That means I might have won!

The stack is getting thinner and thinner. I can see there are only three stories left. Then only two. Mine is one of them! And then she stops at my desk and puts my story on top of it.

I crumble inside, a loser—again. I look at the grade. It's a B+ written in red ink, like a splash of blood, and under it is a comment: *Your writing is good, but you didn't follow instructions, Andy. Please see me after class.*

I feel so rotten I can hardly stand it.

Ms. Soto goes to the head of the class and sits on the edge of her desk. "First, I want to say what a fine job you *all* did." She smiles her nicest smile. "There were so many good pieces of writing that you really made it tough on me to pick a winner. But our writer of the month is"— Mrs. Soto smiles and pauses for effect— "Paula Meyers, for her very moving narrative, 'Snowflakes in Summer.'"

"All right, Paula!" her friend Wendy Larson exclaims.

"'*Snowflakes in Summer?*'" says somebody in the back of the room. "What kind of title is that?"

Paula is blushing, and everyone starts commenting on the story even before Ms. Soto clears her voice in preparation to read the stupid thing.

Me, I'm dying inside. I can't stand it. Before I even realize what I'm doing, I jump up and shout, "It's not fair!"

"Andy!" Ms. Soto exclaims. "Sit *down*, please."

"But *my* story is the best one," I tell her, starting to lose control, my chin quivering. "I put so much hard work into it. You just don't know how much it means to me."

"Sit down, jerk," Ted Rosenbloom sneers.

"You're a loser," Bob Prentice jeers. "Face it."

I just stand there like an idiot.

Ms. Soto takes a few steps in my direction. "Sit

down, Andy, *please*," she says, trying to sound calm. She has a funny expression on her face, not like she's mad but like she's worried. "We'll discuss this after class, all right?"

I look around the room, my arms crossed on my chest, my face bright red with embarrassment. I'm about to say okay and sit down, I'm even about to apologize, when all of a sudden I hear my friend Jack Lewis speak up for me.

"Maybe it *isn't* fair," he says. "I mean, maybe Andy's story *is* better than Paula's. How about letting him read it, Ms. Soto, and let the class decide?"

Ted Rosenbloom laughs at first, then agrees with Jack. "Yeah," he says. "Let the nerd read his story."

Now Ms. Soto *is* mad. "That's enough, Ted." She looks at me with a kind of helpless expression on her face. "Andy, I'm sorry. Your story *is* quite good, but it's just too scary. I think—well, for other reasons, too—it's best you don't read it."

Right away everybody picks up on how Ms. Soto is waffling. It's not like her, but she seems flustered and unsure of herself, and the whole class starts to take advantage of the moment.

"I like scary stuff," Osvaldo Torres pipes up. He's a guy with a giraffelike neck who everyone is always making fun of.

"I like it, too," someone else says.

And then kids all over the room start making comments. "It's only fair to hear both stories," one kid says. "Yeah, we should be the judge," says another.

I slump down into my seat. I feel all mixed-up and self-conscious and wish I could crawl away and hide somewhere.

"Chickening out?" Ted taunts me. "Aren't you even going to argue your own case, or are you afraid your writing is so bad you'll become the laughingstock of the whole class?"

"Come on," says this new girl whose name I don't even know. "You said it was so good. Read it."

Finally Ms. Soto gives in. "Would you like to read it, Andy?" she asks me, her brow furrowed but her voice gentle. "You don't have to if you don't want to."

Every eye in the class is on me. My lips are twitching as though they're only loosely attached to my face. I look at my story in my hand. Then I look at all the faces looking at me. Everybody's waiting to see what I'll do.

I'm all set to run away, but instead I say, "The title of my story is 'Mr. X,'" and before I know it, I hear my voice carrying out over the classroom. It's like it's not a part of me, and my lips are moving all on their own. Even my body doesn't feel real, especially my hands. They're trembling so much I can barely turn the pages.

But somehow I manage to keep going, and as I read I hear a few comments being whispered, like "Gross," "Cool," and "Yuck."

My eyes continue to zigzag back and forth across the sentences, and the words just keep coming out of me. As I read on, all the whispered remarks stop and the class becomes completely silent except for the sound of my voice. I don't even have to look up to know that everybody's staring at me like a bunch of zombies. They're scared, or at least they seem to be. And I'm starting to feel good, more confident about my writing.

I read, faster and faster. Then, as I come to the end, I slow down for effect. I read the last few sentences and finally come to the last word. The room is dead silent. Then I say "The End" and sit down.

Giraffe-neck Osvaldo gives me a thumbs up. "You write pretty good," he says. "That's righteously sick stuff."

"Made me want to throw up," Chad Oyama says. "That part about the freezer and the blood and embalming fluid. . . ." His voice trails off and he shakes his head. "Too much for me, man."

Bob Prentice raises his hand. "It didn't even follow the assignment guidelines, Ms. Soto," he says. "I mean, it was good, in a way, but it—"

"Excuse me, Bob." Ms. Soto puts up her hand. "Let's save our comments until after I've read Paula's story." She picks up her reading glasses off her desk and heads toward the wooden lectern in front of the chalkboard. She seems kind of upset, kind of nervous, but she goes ahead and starts reading anyway.

I have to admit that "Snowflakes in Summer" is pretty well written, but I can hardly listen to Ms. Soto read it. I'm busy listening to people whispering about my story, or rather, about me.

"I always thought he was weird," Ilene Gentry whispers to Chad Oyama.

"He gives me the creeps," hisses a voice somewhere behind me.

I start to feel all horrible and squirmy, like I'm a snake; a snake that wants to crawl out of the room and never come back.

"Don't be cruel," Lashonda Casey says real soft. "There's obviously something wrong with him."

I look across the room at my friend Jack Lewis. But he looks away, as though he's embarrassed to have ever been my friend. It's like all of a sudden he's worried that people will think he's like me; nervous and weird, an outcast.

I hear paper crinkle. I hear Ms. Soto reading Paula's story. And I hear someone crying.

And I realize it's me.

* * *

I'm walking down the street, almost halfway home from school, before I realize I still have Ms. Soto's wooden hall pass in my hand. I'm thinking back over what happened. "Andy's crying," someone said. That's when Ms. Soto stopped reading Paula's story, walked over to my seat, and handed me the hall pass.

"Would you like to go to the boys' room?" she asked, giving me a pat on the back. I just started crying harder. Then I ran from the room, leaving all my books and my story behind. But I didn't care. I just had to get out of there.

Now, in the distance, I hear the school bell ring. I look at my watch. It's three o'clock. School just let out, and me, I'm already almost home.

I dry my eyes and my cheeks with my sleeve. People are staring at me as I walk through the main part of town. There are some guys in front of the barber shop, and they see the hall pass, and one of them makes a snide comment. I cringe and just keep walking faster.

Finally I'm about three blocks from my house and a police car comes around the corner, real slow. My hair stands on end. The cop is looking me over, like he's suspicious or something. I feel like a criminal, not just for being out of school, but for everything.

I keep walking like nothing is wrong, and before I know it I'm on my block, and the cop turns down another street. I breathe a sigh of relief until I realize I can't go home yet. My mom will already be home from work, and she'll wonder why I'm out of school so early. I walk back the way I came, then around the block, stalling until it's the right time for me to get there.

At last I feel like it's okay for me to head to my house. When I get there, my mom is in the front yard, watering the lawn. I wave nonchalantly, and she waves back, but there's a funny look on her face.

"Hi, Mom," I say, sure the school has called to tell her that her son is a fugitive.

"Andy," she says, "how come you're coming home from the wrong direction?"

"Huh?" I ask, and then I realize what she's talking about. By going around the block, I ended up walking toward the house from the opposite direction than I normally do. "How was your day?" I ask, trying to get more time to think of an excuse.

"And how come you're carrying that?" my mom wants to know. She's acting like some kind of detective or something.

"Carrying what?" I ask.

She points at the hall pass in my hand.

The blood rushes to my face. I open my mouth to say something, but all that comes out is a sob.

"Andy, honey?" my mom says, looking all confused. "Sweetheart, what's wrong?"

I race inside, run into my room, and slam the door. A few seconds later I hear my mom talking to me through the door, asking me if something bad happened to me at school.

"No," I tell her. "I just don't feel well. I think I'll take a nap before dinner."

My mom starts to press me to tell her what's bothering me, but I cut her short. "Come on, Mom," I say. "I'm just tired, okay?"

She finally gives in, and I lie down on my bed, close my eyes, and pretend to sleep.

* * *

I guess my pretend sleep turned into a real sleep, because about an hour later I wake up from a really weird dream. I was writing, and words were leaking out of my pen like drops of dark red blood.

"Bizarre," I whisper, still groggy from my dream.

Then from somewhere in the house I hear voices, followed by footsteps coming toward my room. By the sound I can tell two people are now outside the door.

"Andy, it's me, honey," says my mom, knocking softly. "Open the door. There's someone here to see you."

"Who?" I grumble.

And when she tells me it's Ms. Soto, I just about drop dead.

"I'm sorry if we woke you," Ms. Soto says through the door. "May I come in?"

"Ms. Soto stopped by on her way home," my mom says. "She tells me you had a little problem in class today. She just wants to talk to you for a moment."

I feel weird and scared to have my teacher in my bedroom, but I finally get up and open the door.

"Do you want to talk about it, honey?" my mom asks, coming into my room with Ms. Soto.

"It's over now," I mumble, wishing I were dead. "There's nothing to talk about."

Ms. Soto gives me a big smile. "May I sit down?"

she asks in a sweet voice.

I want to tell her no. Instead I say, "Sure."

"Andy," she says, sitting down in my desk chair, "I know that you were upset at not being picked as writer of the month, and I came here to explain why."

"Why?" I ask, so embarrassed I could scream.

"You got a B plus on your story," Ms. Soto starts in, "but you would have gotten an A if you had followed the guidelines. It was supposed to be a *nonfiction* narrative, not a work of fiction."

I don't have anything to say to this. If I tell her it's a true story, that it isn't fiction, she won't believe me. So I just look at her and say nothing.

"I also noticed that you seemed very tired in class," Ms. Soto goes on. "Have you been under a lot of stress lately?"

I just shrug.

"Ms. Soto was also a little worried about the contents of your story," my mom pipes in. "She told me it was about a boy that goes out at night and does horrible things." She looks at my teacher. "What sorts of horrible things?" she asks Ms. Soto.

"It's a bit like Mary Shelley's *Frankenstein*," Ms. Soto explains. "In Andy's story, the main character sneaks out at night, steals body parts from a dissecting room, then makes a living monster out of them."

"Why would you want to write about something like *that*?" my mom asks, wrinkling up her nose in disgust.

But before I can say anything, Ms. Soto starts in again.

"I was bothered when I first read the story, and I became even more concerned when I remembered something I read in the newspaper the other day." She looks at my mom. "I don't know if there's any connection, but yesterday there was a short article on a back page of the newspaper about a break-in at Byrne Medical School."

"What?!" my mom exclaims, the word coming out in a puzzled gasp.

That's where I got the idea from, I feel like telling them. But I decide to just let them think whatever they want and just look at them with a blank expression on my face.

Ms. Soto frowns. "Andy," she says with a funny edge to her voice, "your story, 'Mr. X,' is so vividly written that it sounds as though you actually experienced it. It—"

"Excuse me, Ms. Soto!" my mom blurts out angrily. "But I think you're off base in accusing my son of something so ghastly!"

I roll my eyes and chuckle to myself. "Well, Ms. Soto," I say, a sarcastic edge to my voice, "I guess you're on to me."

"Andy," Ms. Soto says, her eyes opening wide, "I hope you're kidding. You *are,* aren't you?"

I shake my head no, but I cover my mouth so she can't see my grin.

"Andy, stop this teasing this instant!" my mom orders me. She doesn't know who to be angry with now.

Ms. Soto reaches into her tote bag and takes out my notebook and school books. "You left these at school today," she says, handing them to me. Then she takes out my story, scans it, and starts to read a passage out loud. "'The boy wiped the sweat from his brow.'"

For effect, I wipe my own brow.

"'He broke into a wide grin—'"

I grin real wide.

"'—then he took the arm out of the plastic bag and

stood there for a moment, studying the severed limb.'"

I study my own arm as if I've never seen it before.

"'Then he put the arm in the old green upright freezer. Soon he would have enough parts to make his monster. He—'"

"Stop this!" my mom almost shouts. Her face has gone all slack and pale.

Ms. Soto is also starting to look real upset, and her brow is all furrowed up with concern. "By any chance," she asks my mom nervously, "do you have an old green upright freezer?"

My mom nods, sort of numblike.

"The story mentions earlier that the freezer is in the basement," Ms. Soto says hesitantly. "Uh, by any chance, do you happen to have a spare freezer in the basement?"

"Yup, and it's green, too," I say proudly.

My mom stares at me, her eyes getting wider and wider. "Oh, Andy!" she says. "You didn't. I mean, you couldn't! You wouldn't!"

I hang my head like I'm guilty. I can feel my mom's eyes drilling holes in my head, and when I look up, I see her hurrying out of the room with Ms. Soto right behind her.

"I know he's just playing with us," my mom is saying as they head down the hall. "That has to be it!"

Knowing that I really have both their imaginations going, I have to stifle a laugh as I follow them down the hall and into the kitchen toward the door to the basement. I can't tell if she's angry or frightened or what as she flings the door open.

As she stomps down the stairs, yanking the cord on the bare-bulb light, she is mumbling something that I can't hear. Ms. Soto and I aren't saying anything. We're just following her down the stairs, lit up now by the bare bulb that's swinging back and forth and casting a strobelike illumination across the dark basement.

It's like an old-time black-and-white movie as my mom makes her way to our spare freezer. Slowly she grips the handle. I can see she's about to scream, and Ms. Soto is looking at me in horror. I look back at her in the flickering half-light, then turn my gaze in the direction of my mom's hand as she pulls the door open.

We all hold our breath as the room fills with the yellowish light from the freezer. Arms and legs, hands and feet, a torso, and a head—that's what they're *afraid* they'll see.

But there's nothing.

Mom lets out a sigh of relief that fills the whole basement. Then Ms. Soto does the same.

We all march back upstairs, and now it's Ms. Soto who is mumbling under her breath. I think she's trying to figure out how to get out of this mess. Anyway, when we get into the kitchen, she has an embarrassed sort of smile on her face. "You really had me going, Andy," she says.

I smile back at her, all innocent.

"It's like I said before," she goes on, sort of fumbling for something to say, "you *are* quite a good writer. The only thing that kept you from winning the contest was that you didn't follow the instructions."

"Well, I thought I did, Ms. Soto," I tell her.

Ms. Soto shakes her head. "It was supposed to be a true-life, first-person narrative, *not* a short story, *not* fiction. You do understand the difference, don't you?"

"Yes," I say flatly.

"Andy," my mom says, "you had me scared out of my wits!"

I decide to play with her a little. "Come on, Mom. Admit it. You actually thought I did what I wrote in my story, didn't you?" I finally have to let out the laughter I've been holding. "Why don't you check under my bed or out in the yard? See if you can find my Frankenstein monster." I'm really laughing now. "Go ahead, Mom. Look in the garage, too."

By this time my mom is laughing with me. "Don't rub it in," she says, trying to get a hold of herself. She looks at Ms. Soto helplessly. "I'm sorry. My son is a real prankster."

Ms. Soto looks like she can't wait to get out of the house. She heads for the front door, and I race ahead and open it for her like a gentleman.

"Well, Andy," she says as she steps out onto the front porch. "I guess I'll see you in class tomorrow." And with that she turns and goes click-clacking in her heels down the front walk.

"See ya!" I call after her, unable to keep a silly grin off my face.

* * *

Mom leaves for work at 5 A.M. the next day. As usual, I get up and make my own breakfast and get ready for school, but I don't leave until after lunch. I take all the back alleyways, down my special, *private* route, and really take my time getting to school. You see, I don't intend to make it there until my last class, Ms. Soto's English class.

At 2:06 I arrive at school, but I hang around until after the bell rings. Then I slip into the building and head down the silent hallway toward my English class. Although I was freaked out in class yesterday, I'm excited about going to class today. I've got something really special for Ms. Soto and the class to see, something, or rather some*one* who will prove that I do know the difference between fiction and nonfiction.

"We have a new student!" I say as I throw open the door and step inside. "Say hello to Mr. X!"

His head a little cockeyed, and his tongue hanging out of his paralyzed-looking mouth, Mr. X walks into the room. Following behind, I can see that I still have some work to do on him. One leg is longer than the other, his arms are too short for his body, and for some reason his shoulders keep moving up and down involuntarily. Still, I can tell by the reaction of the class—*and* Ms. Soto—that they're very impressed with my creation by the way they are all staring.

"See," I tell everyone. "I did the writing assignment the way I was sup—"

But I have to stop for a moment. Mr. X has wandered off, and I have to go take him by the hand and lead him back to the front of the class. "You'll have to excuse my friend," I say, blushing a little. "His brain doesn't work very well yet."

As if to prove my point, Mr. X lets go of my hand and limps away. I feel guilty looking at his mismatched legs. When I stole them from the medical school, I was in such a rush I didn't realize they weren't from the same body. He looks as though he's in pain now, and as though he's going to fall down any minute as he goes clomping down an aisle.

I catch up with him and guide him back down a row of terrified-looking students. We stand together in front of the class, not too far from the door, just in case anyone decides to leave. I want their full attention and I think I have it. In fact, everyone looks kind of frozen in their seats.

"This is Mister X," I begin again. "It was real fun making him in the shed behind my house for our writing assignment."

I pause for a moment. Everyone seems to be coming alive, everyone but Ms. Soto. While some kids are crying and some are fidgeting like they're going to make a run for it, she's just sitting behind her desk with her jaw practically in her lap.

I start to talk again, real loud this time, since there seems to be a lot of noise developing in the room. "Mr. X is made from the corpses of people who—"

Again, I have to stop. I frown at the class to show my annoyance. How in the world am I supposed to talk when everybody is running around and screaming? I mean, it's enough to drive a guy nuts!

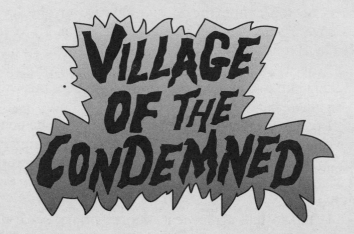

VILLAGE OF THE CONDEMNED

*R*obert and Brenda Turner, thirteen-year-old twins, had been traveling all summer around the east with their folks in a motor home. It was September, and Nashua Trailer Park on the outskirts of Charlesburg, Massachusetts, would be their last stop before heading home to Connecticut. The idea of summer being over, and of school starting, was definitely *not* something the twins were looking forward to.

Robert was grumpy. He'd overslept that morning, and when he got up and found that his parents and Brenda had gone off somewhere without him, he was really annoyed. Yawning, trying to wake himself up, he stumbled into the kitchen, poured himself a bowl of cereal, and went to eat outside.

He had just finished eating and was sitting on the pull-down metal step of their motor home, tying the laces of his sneakers, when he heard his name being called from down the dirt road.

"Hey, Robert!" Brenda was yelling as she pedaled her bike around a bend. "Wake up, lazy bones!" She coasted by six or seven motor homes in the trailer park before coming to a squeaking stop in front of the shiny silver one her parents had rented for the summer.

"What's up?" Robert asked, getting up from the step. "You look all excited."

Brenda, her baseball cap on backward and wearing aviator sunglasses, hopped off her bike. "I just heard about this weird place and we *have* to go there."

"Where do we *have* to go?" Robert asked, trying to shake his grumpiness but not being very successful.

"It's a village not far from here," Brenda said, ignoring his attitude. "And the people there turn into worms, have spider blood in their veins, and—"

"Yeah, right!" Robert scoffed. "And who told you this?"

"An old blind lady in Charlesburg, down by the lake," Brenda answered. "I was sitting on a bench beside her, and she just started up a conversation. It turns out that she's lived in Charlesburg all her life and—"

"Wake me when you get to the interesting part," Robert interrupted, punctuating his sentence with a big yawn.

"Anyway," Brenda went on, paying no attention to her brother's wisecrack, "we talked about a lot of things, and I happened to mention that you and I were thinking of going on a hike today."

"So?" said Robert with a shrug.

"So she told me there were rumors of strange people living in the woods and that we should stay clear of a place called Deadface Cliff. Supposedly these strange people live right by it."

71

"So naturally you want to go there?" Robert asked matter-of-factly.

"No, I want *us* to go."

"What about Mom and Dad?" Robert wanted to know.

"They're in town shopping. We can bike out to this place and be back in a couple of hours."

"Well, I guess visiting with a few spider-blood people would be more interesting than hanging around here," Robert said. "I'll go get my bike."

* * *

At first there were trails through the dogwoods, ferns, and forests of birch and maple. Then the trails gave way to tangles of vegetation mixed with gnarled, twisted trees. Soon Brenda and Robert had to abandon their bikes and continue on foot. For a while the going wasn't too difficult, but then the ground became all muddy, and they found themselves sloshing along a meandering stream. Leaving the stream bed, they headed into a field of tall grass, the damp blades swiping at them, soaking them up to their calves.

"Brenda, where are we going?" Robert complained as the sun blazed down. He was soaked practically head to toe from both the wet vegetation and his own sweat.

Sun glinting off her sunglasses, Brenda looked back at her brother. "The old lady said there's a cliff that looks like there's a dead man's face carved on it. That's what we're looking for."

"I thought she was blind," Robert commented. "How would she know what it looks like?"

Brenda shrugged and trudged on.

Ahead, the tall grass began to thin and the ground

descended abruptly into a heavily wooded area. Overhead, the trees had grown into a canopy of intertwining, snakelike branches, while underfoot was a thick carpeting of soggy, moldering leaves.

"This place gives me the creeps," Robert mumbled.

Brenda nodded in agreement. "Me, too," she said. "Want to head back? We've gone farther than I thought we'd have to go and haven't seen a thing."

Robert looked around for a moment, then hopped over a narrow stream. "Let's keep going for a while," he said. "We've come this far, we might as well look a little longer."

The light grew fainter as they moved through the forest. Rounding a large boulder, they came upon a wide sunken area of dead and dying trees. As they were picking their way through jumbles of rotted trunks and twisted branches, a girl came into view. She seemed to be floating in midair!

Speechless, Robert and Brenda stared at the delicate, pretty girl, who wore a long old-fashioned-looking dress of blue velvet. She stared back at them, seeming to be as frightened and confused as they were.

Brenda grabbed hold of Robert and whispered, "Is she a ghost?"

Robert was about to say he didn't have a clue *what* they were looking at when the girl suddenly started to drift backward. She then whirled around in the air, floated down to the ground, and began running away from them as soon as her feet touched the dirt. Robert and Brenda stared at her as she disappeared into dense forest. Then they looked at each other. "Let's get out of here!" they yelled in unison.

But as they turned to run, the two kids stopped in

horror when they found a bear coming toward them. Screaming in fright and then struck dumb with amazement, the two kids just stood there watching as the bear instantly changed into a bearded man dressed in dark clothing right before their eyes.

"What's going on?" Robert whispered as he and Brenda backed away.

"I don't have any—"

But just then Brenda bumped into something. She whirled around to find the girl floating right behind her.

"I am sorry, Father," she said, addressing the man as she stepped lightly to earth.

"Speak not, Rachel," the man said sternly. "Do not compound your error by asking forgiveness. By your recklessness, you have imperiled our safety, as well as that of these two young wanderers."

The pretty girl hung her head.

"Who are you?" Brenda managed to ask as she looked back and forth between the man and the girl.

"What are you going to do with us?" Robert asked, his voice a strangled-sounding whisper.

The man looked to his daughter. "They will have to die, Rachel, as we did."

"No, Father," the girl cried.

"It is the law!"

"A law only the council of elders may impose, Father!" the girl begged.

The man frowned, then slowly nodded his head. "Very well," he said, fixing his blue eyes on the now shaking kids. "Let the elders decide." And with that his blue eyes turned liquid black . . . and so did Robert and Brenda's world as the power emanating from the man's eyes stunned them, engulfed them, causing their legs to give way as they crumbled unconscious to the ground.

* * *

Dizzy, Brenda awoke to find herself lying on the rough-hewn floor of a shack. On hands and knees she crawled to where her still-unconscious brother lay in the corner. "Robert," she whispered. "Wake up."

"Where are we? What happened to us?" Robert asked, slowly coming to. He rubbed his eyes, still groggy. "Who were those people? *What* were those people?"

Brenda shook her head, unable to offer any sort of explanation. She peered out through a gap between the boards of the shack. It offered her only a slicelike view of a village. "This is weird," she said, gazing at the villagers, most of whom walked with heavy, flat-footed steps, as though trying to stay earth-bound. She caught a glimpse of two little boys running and playing. Suddenly they levitated and were chasing one another through the air.

"Nathaniel! Zachariah!" A middle-aged woman wearing a white bonnet and short white apron over a brown velvet dress stamped her foot. "Return thyselves to Earth at once! Didst thou learn nothing from what became of Rachel Smith for her foolishness?"

The boys, looking repentant, descended.

Looking on, a little girl who suddenly transformed herself into a snake, coiled downward. "You're bad boys!" hissed the little girl's voice from the snake's mouth. "You're going to get into trouble!"

"As are you, Esther!" snapped the woman. "Change thyself back immediately!"

The little girl did as she was told, then the three

children were marched away out of Brenda's view.

"These people look and talk like Pilgrims or something," Brenda said. "But the things they do make it seem like they're—"

She stopped herself as a hand came through the wall. It belonged to Rachel Smith, who suddenly emerged through the wall entirely and stepped into the room.

Robert and Brenda backed away, gaping in disbelief.

"Do not be alarmed," Rachel said gently. She smiled, blinking her emerald green eyes.

"Wh—what's go-going on?" Robert stammered.

"Who are you people?" Brenda asked.

"We mean thee no ill will," Rachel replied. "We only wish to live in peace."

"Then why are you holding us prisoner?" Robert demanded.

"It is necessary," Rachel said matter-of-factly. "You are a threat to us, to our privacy."

"What do you mean?" Brenda asked.

"We are always in danger, and our existence has been threatened ever since we came—"

"Came from where?" Robert interrupted.

"From Cadmus, a place much like your Earth."

Brenda stared at the girl. Except for her dress, she looked like a normal human being. "Are you trying to tell us you're aliens?"

"We came in your year of 1674," Rachel replied softly, "adopted your customs and way of living, then settled in the township of Salem, hoping only to live in harmony and peace."

"*Salem?*" Robert asked. "You mean Salem, *Massachusetts?*"

The girl nodded. "Yes, and for many years we concealed our powers of levitation, mind-reading, changing bodily form, and so forth. We wanted to fit in with your world," she said sadly. "But blunders were made, such as our meeting in the woods today, and many Earthlings became frightened."

"When we met in the woods today," Brenda said, "you flew."

"Levitated," corrected the green-eyed girl. "And it is this simple power which has caused us the most grief over the ages."

"Salem is where they said there were witches," Robert said. "They said those people could fly."

Rachel nodded again. "One of our forefathers, who had taken the Earth name Burroughs, was seen levitating in his own home, and his stepchild, in play, took the form of a cat. News spread quickly. The hysteria began and . . ." Rachel shrugged. "Well, the rest is written in your history books."

"You're talking about the Salem witchcraft trials," Robert said in disbelief.

"Yes, that is what your history books called them. We simply call them the Dark Days."

"And so all the stuff in the history books, the whole thing about witches"— Robert turned to Brenda, a look of excitement on his face— "was all wrong!"

"So what you're telling us, Rachel, is that the people of Salem thought your people, who are actually aliens, were witches," Brenda said in awe.

"We prefer to be called Cadmunes, not aliens," Rachel said, smiling. "But, yes, that is what I am telling you."

Robert frowned, deep in thought. "But why would your people want to . . ."

"Come to Earth?" Rachel asked, her eyes twinkling as she read Robert's mind. "Our planet was dying. Great hydrogen fires were burning up our atmosphere, and we knew we must escape in order to survive." For a moment she looked sad. "Unfortunately only nineteen managed to escape to Earth. The others . . ." Her voice trailed off.

Robert studied Rachel as if seeing her for the first time. "In Salem," he said slowly, "did your people at least try to explain where you were from?"

"Some did, but that only increased the madness and disbelief." Rachel sighed. "No one would listen, and soon the trials, and the executions, began. Those of our ancestors who were not found out fled into these woods, and we have been here ever since, in hiding." A confident smile broke onto her face. "In our four-hundred-year history, we have been discovered only eleven times."

"And what happens to those who discover you?" Brenda asked, fear welling up within her.

Rachel hung her head. When she looked up, tears were brimming in her eyes. "It is all my fault," she cried. "If only I had not done that which is—"

"What do your people do with those who discover you?" Robert demanded.

"The council of elders is now meeting to decide your fate," Rachel finally said, pausing. "You see, over the years we have grown hard and . . ." A tear slipped from her eye.

"But they wouldn't kill us!" Robert exclaimed. "Would they?"

Rachel nodded, tears now coursing down her cheeks. "Intruders are put to death," she said simply.

For a moment the three fell into silence, then Rachel said she must go. But before she stepped back through the wall, she warned Brenda and Robert that it would do no good to try to escape. "My people can see you through the walls, read your every thought, and change themselves into whatever they please. Do not add to your misery by fighting things you cannot control."

Still, after Rachel left, Robert beat his fists on the thick, coarse walls until his hands were bruised and bloody. And both he and Brenda cried for help until their throats were raw.

Finally, realizing it was hopeless, Brenda put her arms around Robert, and they sat down together on the floor, awaiting their fate.

* * *

The villagers came for them at dusk. The door flew open, and men in dark clothing entered the one-room shack.

"Come with us now," Rachel's father ordered.

"What are you going to do to us?" Brenda demanded.

"A verdict of death has been rendered."

Brenda and Robert backed away in horror.

"But we don't mean you any harm," Brenda pleaded.

"You will come with us now," one of the other men said.

"No!" Robert shouted. "We're not going anywhere!"

But even as Robert spoke, some unearthly force took hold of him and Brenda. Together, the two kids began to walk out of the shack, their legs moving woodenly as they stumbled out into the gathering gloom of night.

In the center of the village the other men, women, and

children stood silently in a large circle, holding torches. In the middle of the circle were two large stakes around which great bundles of wood and straw had been piled.

Robert cried. Brenda screamed. But their legs continued to move on their own, taking them right into the circle toward their doom. Then, with all eyes upon them, both kids, still not operating under their own powers but under some unseen force, pressed their backs involuntarily against the stakes.

Rachel's father stepped forward solemnly. Near him on the ground lay two long, heavy lengths of chain. He looked at them, and as he did, the lengths of chain rose from the ground and glided toward Robert and Brenda. Then suddenly, like black metal snakes, they wrapped around the kids in a blur of motion, binding Brenda and Robert to the stakes.

"Why are you doing this?" Brenda cried.

"You must die as did our ancestors," Rachel's father said in a rumbling voice. "We must rid ourselves of you so that our people may live in security and peace, unknown and unbothered by Earthlings who would destroy us."

Suddenly Rachel Smith broke from the circle of people and ran to her father. "Please, Father," she begged.

"Begone, child!" he ordered.

"No, Father," she cried. "They did no wrong. They are but children!"

"Children who would tell others about our village," he replied sternly. "Then once again our people would be persecuted unjustly."

"Is what you intend less evil than that which was done to our people?" Rachel asked. "If so, burn me as well!" And with that, Rachel suddenly planted herself in front of her father, her green eyes glistening in the light of the fiery torches. "I am to blame that these Earthlings found us," she declared, "and I do not wish to live if you would put them to death for my foolishness."

"Rachel speaks wisely," said a voice from the circle. A murmur of assent filled the air. There were grumbles of disagreement, which were drowned out by stronger voices, voices calling for the lives of the two children to be spared.

Finally, one by one, the torches were extinguished. "Very well," Rachel's father said as the chains magically unwound from Brenda and Robert and dropped to the ground with a clatter. Numb, the two children stepped forward.

"Thank you, Rachel," Brenda whispered.

"We'll never forget you for this," Robert added, smiling.

"But that is what you *must* do," Rachel insisted. "Now go in peace, and tell no one of us, or of what you have seen and heard. I will not ask you for a promise, but only to think about the trust we are placing in you. Go, my friends."

* * *

Brenda and Robert spoke little as they made their way through the dark woods. Every once in a while they looked back and thought that it had all been no more than a very bad dream. Then, off in the distance, they heard a *thwacking* sound, faint at first, then louder and louder, reverberating through the woods.

"What's that?" asked Brenda, and then suddenly a great spear of blue-white light pierced downward through the blackness, moving across the landscape.

"It's a helicopter!" Robert exclaimed. "They've come looking for us!"

Together, he and Brenda scrambled up onto a narrow, grass-covered plateau and waved their arms, yelling and screaming for help.

The beam of light moved backward across the landscape, passed over them, then returned, bracketing them in sudden brilliance.

"Stand back," boomed a voice over a loudspeaker from the hovering craft. Then a moment later, in a whirlwind of dust and flying debris, the helicopter settled to the ground.

"Robert and Brenda Turner, I assume," the middle-aged woman at the controls of the craft said, flashing a grin to the children who scrambled aboard.

"Yeah!" Robert exclaimed. "And are we glad to see you!"

"Let's get you two home," the pilot said, already throttling back. "Your parents are very worried."

The chopper rose vertically, then drifted in a sweeping arc back down through the canyon, its single powerful light illuminating the woods below. For a moment the village came into view.

"What's that?" the woman asked, pointing toward the village.

The searchlight danced over the roofs of the cottages, then the chopper veered left in the opposite direction.

Brenda and Robert just looked at each other, then shrugged.

"Base one, this is Rescue Four," the pilot said into a handset. "Returning to base with two healthy but tired-looking kids!"

"Good work, Rescue Four!" squawked a man's voice through the handset.

"And I've spotted something out here," said the pilot. "Looks like people are living out here in a village I didn't know existed." The pilot glanced at Robert and Brenda as she headed on a line over the dark landscape. "The sheriff may want to investigate. Something's going on out here, and I think these kids may know what it is."

* * *

The next day the sheriff's office conducted an air-search for the peculiar town that seemed to have sprung up in the middle of the woods. The pilot of the small plane zigzagged over the general area where the lost children had been found but was unable to locate the village the chopper pilot had reported seeing.

The search was abandoned. But news of it sparked old rumors about a bunch of strange people living deep in the woods, rumors that had circulated off and on for over a century in Charlesburg.

A town meeting was held, and after some discussion, the townspeople decided action would have to be taken. They talked themselves into believing the strange people were dangerous, and by the end of the meeting it was agreed that a ground-search of the area was needed.

Two days later, on a Saturday morning, a group of forty men armed with shotguns, handguns, and baseball bats set off into the woods. Robert and Brenda were "asked" to join them, and did so only against their will.

"Where were you kids when you were found?" Brenda and Robert were repeatedly asked as they trekked through the woods.

The kids gave only vague, misleading answers. "Over that hill, I think," Robert would say, scratching his head. And after leading the group over the hill, Brenda would frown and tell them that her brother was all wrong, that the area in which they had been lost was off in a completely different direction.

"I don't think these kids know anything," a balding, shotgun-toting man complained.

"Or maybe they're just playing games with us," said the Charlesburg Bank manager who had appointed himself the leader. He assembled the group and announced, "These kids are leading us on a wild-goose chase. And the one place they seem to keep leading us away from is Deadface Cliff."

"Then I say that that's where we go," the owner of a Charlesburg gas station suggested.

Robert and Brenda lagged behind as the ragged expedition continued on through the woods. Soon, looming through the trees, Deadface Cliff came into view below.

"Hey!" someone called, standing atop a stone outcropping. "There it is!"

The group hurried through the dense forest and emerged into a clearing at the foot of the cliff. There they came upon the village, but it was totally abandoned.

Everyone fanned out, searching dwelling after dwelling, but all were empty.

"Well, this was a waste of time," grumbled a potbellied man leaning against the shack that had once imprisoned Robert and Brenda. "There isn't a soul here."

Brenda and Robert just stood there grinning. Robert saw a lizard sunning itself on a fallen branch and pointed it out to Brenda. She nodded knowingly, then spotted a threesome of chipmunks chattering nearby.

"What are you two so happy about?" the leader of the group asked, coming up behind Robert and Brenda who were smiling broadly. "You're holding something back, aren't you?"

"Why would we do that?" Robert responded innocently.

"I don't know," he said suspiciously. "I only know that you two have been leading us in circles."

"That's not so," Brenda said emphatically. She turned her gaze upward to a crow perched on the branch of a tree. The crow had emerald green eyes. "It isn't so at all. Trust me."

The man walked away, muttering.

"Trust me," Brenda said again, looking at the bird and not at the man.

The crow nodded its head, blinked its green eyes, and then took flight, soaring upward into a bright azure sky.

SNAPSHOTS OF THE DEAD

*T*anya Fields had never known her biological parents. At the age of one year she literally had been found on the doorstep of Jessica and Isaac Fields in Petersburg, Virginia. The couple could not have their own children, and for them, the appearance one night of the baby girl, in a finely crafted basket on their doorstep, was truly a miracle.

A neighbor reported that a strange-looking, dark-skinned man in a robe had left the baby on the doorstep, but all efforts to locate him, and the parents of the infant, were unsuccessful. Two years later, after endless red tape, Isaac and Jessica Fields adopted Tanya, and the child legally became their own.

Tanya, a sensitive, intelligent girl, was also quite beautiful. Her flawless skin was a tawny brown, her hair was straight and almost black, and her brown eyes were large, gentle, and mysterious-looking. Fondly, her parents called her "princess."

But suddenly, when Tanya was eleven, her mother died, and both she and her father were devastated. Two years later Isaac Fields, a petroleum engineer for Chemco Oil, was promoted to a new position, one which required him to travel a great deal. And so he enrolled Tanya in the Lamont Boarding School, where she lived nine months of each year.

At first this arrangement was very hard on Tanya, but the three months of the summer that she spent with her dad were always so exciting that they made up for her not seeing him as often as she'd have liked. Usually they were off in some foreign country. Already she'd been to Scotland, Israel, Saudi Arabia, and Romania. But Egypt, where she had gone this summer, was turning out to be the strangest and most interesting place of all.

Despite the poverty and the scorching heat, Egypt seemed a magical place to Tanya. She and her dad had spent their first three days in Cairo, on tours to see the Sphinx and the Great Pyramids. On their fourth day they were going to go to the temple of Rameses II at Abu Simbel, but her dad was needed at work and would be tied up in business meetings all day.

Tanya, it was decided, would spend the day at the Cairo Antiquities Museum. It was just a few blocks from their hotel, the Cairo Hilton.

"You can spend as much time there as you want," her dad told her as they drove together in a taxi to the museum. "But as soon as you're done, I want you to get into a cab and go straight back to the hotel. Agreed?"

"Don't be such a worrywart, Dad!" Tanya exclaimed, pushing her long dark hair back from her forehead. "I'm fourteen. I can take care of myself."

"Princess," her father said gently, "fourteen is really not quite as old as you may think. It can be dangerous for a young girl to be alone in a foreign country. Just do as I ask, okay?"

Rolling her eyes, she nodded.

"Promise?"

"Yes, Dad," Tanya finally said with a laugh. "I promise."

The battered salmon-colored taxi squealed to stop, and the driver looked over the seat at them. "The Museum of the Antiquities," he announced, his tone strangely ominous.

Her dad went on with his lecture on safety, but his words were a blur to Tanya. She was focused on the cab driver. There was something odd about the man. He seemed to be in his twenties, but his eyes were old. In contrast to his healthy deep-brown skin, his eyes were an opaque, time-faded blue.

As Tanya continued to stare at the man, her father passed his hand in front of her eyes. "Princess? Are you listening to me?"

Tanya snapped to attention. "Sorry, Dad," she mumbled. "I was just—"

"Never mind. Just listen for a moment," he said, sounding a little annoyed. "My meeting will be over at four, and I'll be back at the hotel no later than five. The offices of Chemco are only about half a mile from here, and you have the number. So, call if you need me for anything, okay?"

"Okay," Tanya said, feeling as though she were breaking out of a trance. She grabbed her camera from the seat, gave her father a kiss on the cheek, and stepped out of the cab. "Don't work too hard," she added, slamming the door.

From the top of the steps of the museum, Tanya watched the salmon-colored taxi disappear into the noisy chaos of Cairo traffic. *Boy, that cab driver was strange,* she thought, making her way into the silent museum.

Her father had given her money to buy a ticket for a guided tour, but Tanya felt a strong need to be on her own. She wandered alone through the vast rooms, past displays of hieroglyphics, artwork, jewelry, and the ancient bodies of mummies, and found everything to be fascinating. But ever since seeing the cab driver, an odd feeling had taken hold of Tanya. In her mind's eye she kept seeing his face, and somehow she felt as though *he* were actually guiding her through the museum.

Suddenly she stopped in front of a glass case containing the mummified corpse of Amenhotep II, a pharaoh who had lived more than three thousand years ago. But it was not the pharaoh's blackened body that interested Tanya. Nor was it the displays of his jewelry and other artifacts of the time. Instead, Tanya was drawn to an old black-and-white photograph in a wood frame on the wall. Like a magnet, it seemed to pull her toward it.

Tanya stared at the photograph. It showed archaeologists and Egyptian workmen standing, with picks and shovels in hand, at the site where the mummy of Amenhotep II had been found.

Interesting, she thought. And then her heart froze. One of the workmen, staring directly at the camera with a half-smile on his face, was the driver of the cab!

"It can't be!" Tanya muttered under her breath. She quickly checked the date on the photograph. It was 1893.

If the cab driver had been there, that would make him over a hundred years old! She shook her head as if trying to clear it. As impossible as it seemed, the cab driver looked the same age in the picture as he had just a short while ago in the cab.

Tanya was still muttering to herself in disbelief when she suddenly heard a voice coming from behind her.

Nearly startled out of her skin, she turned to find a heavy-set woman in the beige-and-green uniform of a museum guard standing behind her. "Are you all right, young lady?" asked the woman, a concerned, curious expression on her face.

Tanya didn't answer. Instead she backed away, turned, and hurried through the museum, going the way she had come. Her heart pounded with each step.

Emerging from the semidark of the museum into the white-hot mid-morning sunshine, Tanya was nearly blinded for a moment. She stood atop the heavy stone steps, flanked by stone statues of the Egyptian goddess Isis, and waited for her eyes to adjust. As they did she was not surprised at what she saw.

Below in the street was the battered salmon-colored taxi, and leaning against it was the strange driver, obviously waiting for her.

"Who are you?" she asked as she approached the man. "What do you want?"

His lips curled back into the same half-grin Tanya had seen on his face in the photograph. Instead of answering her, he merely reached inside his loose-fitting white robe and took out a crumpled but shiny piece of paper. Silently he handed it to Tanya.

Her hands trembling, Tanya studied the paper,

surprised that the writing on it was in English. It appeared to be some kind of advertisement: *Visit the ancient city of Iunu,* it said. *Enjoy the wonders of the past.*

Apprehensive and completely baffled, Tanya was about to hand the paper back when the man suddenly opened the passenger door of the cab. "Come," he said, his voice soft and melodious. "Come, please." He gestured for her to get into the cab.

Frightened, Tanya backed away. Then, clutching the piece of paper in one hand and her camera in the other, she ran, not stopping until she reached the hotel.

* * *

Panting, out of breath, with beads of perspiration glistening on her face, Tanya pushed past a startled doorman and ran through the lobby of the hotel. Guests and hotel employees turned their heads to stare at her. Embarrassed, she slowed herself to a walk and made her way to the registration desk. An unsmiling balding little man came to the counter.

"May I help you?" he asked.

Tanya unfolded the piece of paper. "Can you tell me what this is about?" she asked. "What exactly is Iunu and where is it?"

The man frowned and shook his head. "I know little of Iunu," he said, "only that the slums of Al-Matariyah are built on its ruins." His face brightened slightly. "But perhaps Adiva, another clerk here at the registration desk, will know."

The paper in hand, he made his way to a petite short-haired young woman.

"This is Adiva Ghali. She attended the university here,"

the bald man said, returning to the counter with the young woman. "Hopefully she can be of assistance."

Tanya thanked the man, then turned her attention to the woman. "Do you know anything about this Iunu place, Miss Ghali?"

Adiva Ghali took the paper and studied it carefully. "Iunu is a long-vanished city where ancient Egyptian mystics studied astronomy and spiritualism," she said. "They were especially fascinated with the mysteries concerning time. Now it's a slum, surrounded by a huge trash dump."

"What do you mean by 'mysteries concerning time'?" Tanya asked.

"I don't know a great deal about it," Miss Ghali answered, smiling modestly. "I know only that the Iunuans believed that the past, present, and future overlap, that they can join as a single moment at certain places on Earth at certain times. Iunu was said to be one of those places." She laughed lightheartedly. "But, of course, that's all nonsense."

"Maybe it's not," Tanya said, thinking about how the cab driver had appeared both in his cab *and* in the century-old photograph in the museum.

The young woman blinked. "Pardon me?"

"Nothing." Tanya forced a smile. "Thanks for the information."

* * *

That evening, over dinner, Tanya told her dad about her strange experience.

"Well," he said, seeming not to take it very seriously, "I'm sure you're mistaken about the photograph. I don't doubt that the taxi driver and the man in the photo looked similar. But honestly, Princess, they couldn't possibly have been the same person. You're just letting your imagination get the better of you."

"Maybe you're right," Tanya admitted. "But do you think we could possibly go to Iunu together tomorrow?"

"Afraid not, honey. I've got another meeting tomorrow, and the day after that we fly to Aswan. Why don't you just spend tomorrow relaxing? Sit out by the pool. Read. Swim a bit." He frowned. "Wish I could spend the day relaxing, instead of being cooped up in boring meetings."

"What are your boring meetings about?" Tanya asked, trying to be polite and show an interest in her dad's work.

He launched into a huge explanation of Chemco's plans for a new refinery, and Tanya pretended to listen attentively. Her mind, however, was elsewhere. It was on how she would get to Iunu in the morning.

* * *

That night, while lying in her bed and staring at the ceiling, Tanya felt sneaky and guilty for planning to go to Iunu without telling her father. But how could she help herself? It was as though she were in the grip of some supernatural force that was practically *forcing* her to go.

As soon as her dad left for Chemco the next morning, Tanya went to talk to Adiva Ghali at the registration desk. The friendly clerk explained that the best and fastest ways to get to Al-Matariyah, the town that now covered the site of the ancient city, would be by taxi or by one of the shuttle vans. But the cost of both was more than forty U.S. dollars, far beyond Tanya's means. All she could afford was one of the local buses.

Boarding one that said "Al-Matariyah" on its signboard, Tanya had no idea of what she was getting herself into. The bus was hot, and it stank of perspiration, carbon monoxide, and bundles of unwrapped food. It was filled to capacity with passengers who boarded not only at scheduled stops but also at every intersection. Tanya could barely breathe there were so many people crowded in with her. In fact, by the time they approached Al-Matariyah and the ruins of Iunu, there were so many passengers that many were perched on the mudguards and clinging perilously to the window and door frames.

From afar the place looked like a typical shantytown, a jumble of ramshackle dwellings built of wooden boxes, corrugated siding, and tin cans pounded flat. As the bus rattled closer Tanya could see that the dwellings were set next to a seemingly endless sprawl of rubbish. Garbage was piled in foul-smelling mounds around all the shacks. Rags, waste paper, rotting vegetation, moldering food containers, and other refuse covered the ground in huge heaps.

Tanya was one of only a handful of people who exited the bus at the awful-looking place. As the bus rumbled away in a cloud of dust and exhaust fumes, she just stood there clutching her camera and wondering why she had come.

She was staring at a sea of trash, holding her nose, fending off air ripe with the stench of rotting garbage, when suddenly she spotted grimy, scarecrowlike people tramping through the debris. They were sorting through the mess and putting various items into piles, obviously looking for things to salvage.

What a terrible way to live! Tanya thought. *I have so much, and these poor people have so little!*

As she watched, a little boy of about ten approached her. He was dressed in a faded green shirt and baggy pants, and he was holding a cardboard box filled with unwrapped pieces of some sort of hard candy. He asked something in Arabic, apparently hoping she would buy some.

Tanya picked out a piece of the candy, then dropped several coins into the boy's outstretched hand. He smiled broadly, and Tanya quickly snapped a picture of him.

As the little boy scurried off, Tanya made her way down winding dirt paths through the seemingly endless mounds of trash. Now and again she snapped a few pictures.

She was about to take a picture of a donkey harnessed to a makeshift cart when it happened.

All at once everything around her began to flicker. The sun flashed across the sky, backward from west to east, giving the impression of going off and on like a strobe light. Day, it seemed, was turning to night, over and over, in rapid, fluttering succession.

"Wh-what's happening?" Tanya cried.

Although she was standing still, she had the feeling of hurtling in reverse through time. It was all happening so fast that she was actually beginning to feel sick to her stomach. Then, as quickly as all the strangeness began, it stopped.

Tanya blinked and stared in disbelief. *Everything* had changed.

Gone were the scavenging people. Gone was the endless vista of garbage. Now the sand was a glistening, pristine white. Palm trees grew, gardens flourished, and in the near distance was a beautiful walled city.

Both curious and frightened, Tanya began making her way through a garden toward the city. Then she stopped abruptly. From somewhere came the steady beat of drums.

Quickly hiding behind a tree, Tanya watched as a portcullis—an iron gate set into the city wall—was raised. Men and women, their heads shaved, emerged. They appeared to be royalty of some sort, and each wore mounds of jewelry. A few even wore what appeared to be artificial gold beards. Slaves shaded these people from the sun with oversized canopies made of palm leaves.

Is it possible? Tanya's mind raced. *Could I have gone back into the past, back to when Iunu was a beautiful city?*

Suddenly remembering that she still had her camera hanging from a strap around her neck, Tanya quickly took picture after picture. "If I ever get back to my own time," she muttered to herself, "I'd better have proof of this."

In awe, Tanya watched as white-robed priests emerged from the open gate, followed by a squad of soldiers flanking a gold coffin, a sarcophagus, carried by slaves. Hunkering down low as the procession passed within yards of her, Tanya could see the gold sarcophagus more clearly. The image of a king, a pharaoh with his arms crossed and holding a scepter, glinted on the lid.

I'm witnessing a burial, she thought, a *royal burial.* Kneeling behind a low wall in the garden, Tanya fed a fresh roll of film into her camera. Then, watching in miniature through the view-finder, she continued to take pictures.

The procession wound its way toward a squat eight-sided burial vault that was in the process of being built. Some of the stones were not yet in place, and nearby a group of craftsmen was hewing an intricate design into a rectangular slab of black stone. It appeared to be a door that would be put in place later.

Wouldn't it be incredible to actually have pictures of what it looks like in the tomb before it's sealed! Tanya thought, wondering how she could get to the vault and slip inside without being noticed. Cautiously she began to move forward on hands and knees, when suddenly her eyes went wide with terror.

Silently watching her, half-concealed in the lush vegetation of the garden, was a man. The hair stood up on the back of her neck and her eyes opened even wider as she recognized his face. It was the cab driver! The same man whose hundred-year-old picture had been on the wall of the museum!

He had an odd, knowing look on his face, and he parted the foliage and approached her.

Stifling a scream, Tanya rose to her feet. "Get away from me!" she warned.

"Do not be afraid," he said.

"Who are you?" Tanya asked, her voice off-key with fear.

"I am Ibrahim, messenger of Mahmoud Sheddadi, who is the King of Iunu." He paused and smiled awkwardly. "The king is your father."

"*My father?*" Tanya gasped.

"At the age of one year I brought you to the doorstep of the people called Fields whom you learned to call your parents."

Her brow furrowing, Tanya thought back to a story her parents had told her of a mysterious dark-skinned man leaving her on their doorstep when she was a baby.

"From Iunu," continued the man, "I stepped through

time and space with you in my arms, as was commanded by my king, so that you, his daughter, could behold the wonders of a future world."

"But why was I brought back?" Tanya asked, her voice shaky.

"Your father was ill," the man explained. "It was his wish to see you one more time before he died, but alas, I was too late." Ibrahim gestured toward the funeral procession near the octagonal opening. "My king, your father, is dead."

"This is insane," Tanya whispered.

Ibrahim shook his head and smiled gently. "In two days' time his tomb shall be sealed. You, as his daughter, may view the body, if you so desire. You may even join him on his dark journey. Or you may stay here with your own kind and live with—"

"No!" Tanya cried. "I want to leave!"

Ibrahim extended his hands, palms upward, toward her. "Are you sure, my princess?"

Tanya backed away. "Yes!" she declared emphatically.

"Very well, then," he said. And as he spoke the sky once more began to flutter. Tanya again felt ill, and now had the sensation of being hurtled forward through time. She stumbled, her arms flailing, and then she fell into a pile of trash.

Dizzy and disoriented, Tanya pushed herself to her feet. She then stared in disbelief at the sea of garbage around her and at the people picking through it. She was back at the site of the ancient city of Iunu, now nothing more than a trash dump.

* * *

The police found Tanya walking along the road to Cairo and returned her to the hotel, where her dad was terribly worried. At first, when they brought her to him, he cried out with relief. But his joy at having her returned safely gradually turned to anger.

"How could you do this to me?" he demanded once they were in their hotel room. "How could you go off on your own like that after all your promises?"

But his anger turned to concern for Tanya's mental well-being when she gave him a rambling, tear-filled account of what she said had happened to her. He was afraid she had suffered some kind of trauma, and he told Tanya that he wanted to take her to a doctor.

But the frightened girl flatly refused. "Just develop the film in my camera," she pleaded with her dad. "You'll see. I'm not losing my mind."

Finally Tanya was able to persuade her father to go with her to the hotel photo shop and have the pictures developed. He even paid an additional fee for one-hour processing, obviously eager to see the photographs himself. They would, he was sure, help prove to her that she had only imagined the things she'd described.

But instead of clearing things up, the pictures only made things more confusing. In fact, they left Tanya's father half-convinced she was telling the truth. And so, because of the pictures and because Tanya begged him to, he agreed to go with her to talk to experts in the field of Egyptology.

The next day he canceled their planned trip to Aswan, and together he and Tanya traveled all over Cairo to see historians, archaeologists, and anthropologists, telling each of them Tanya's story and showing them her photographs. Most treated Tanya like a deranged child and her father like an overindulgent parent . . . until they met with Dr. Miriam Hagatha, Director of Archaeological Research at Cairo University.

"You're my last hope," Tanya said as she and her dad settled into chairs across from the desk of the stout bespectacled woman.

"Last hope for what, young lady?" Dr. Hagatha asked.

Nervously Tanya explained what had happened to her, what she had seen, and what she had been told by the strange man who called himself Ibrahim. Then she spread the photographs on the Dr. Hagatha's desk.

"These are pictures of a funeral procession," Tanya explained. "They are burying a king named Mahmoud Sheddadi who lived and died *thousands* of years ago." She paused for a moment to let this sink in. "Anyway, my point is that all these are pictures of something that took place *before* the camera was even invented!"

Dr. Hagatha's eyebrows rose with interest, and Tanya went on, growing more and more agitated by the minute. "At Al-Matariyah, I must have stepped through a time warp or something. Do you see what I'm getting at, Dr. Hagatha? I'm convinced that I was born centuries ago at Iunu. Yesterday I returned to the past and witnessed the funeral procession of my birth father." Tanya looked at the woman across from her directly in the eyes. "I know it sounds crazy, Dr. Hagatha. It sounds crazy to me, too. But I took pictures of the whole thing, pictures that are right there on your desk."

Dr. Hagatha studied the pictures more carefully. "The prints appear to be new," she said, "but the photographs do indeed seem to be of an event that occurred in the distant past." She pushed her glasses higher on her nose. "The pictures look like a place near Khafre's causeway, a remnant of the wall that once enclosed the city of Iunu. However, very little of this twelve-mile-long wall still exists, and virtually nothing remains of the city itself."

"Maybe it's buried by sand and garbage," suggested Tanya.

"Perhaps," muttered Dr. Hagatha, sounding unconvinced. She locked eyes with Tanya. "And you stated a moment ago that the supposed king's name was Mahmoud Sheddadi?"

"Yes," Tanya said with certainty in her voice. "I probably didn't pronounce it correctly, but that was the name."

"Well," Dr. Hagatha said, sitting back in her chair, "there is no mention of a king by that name in any work I've ever encountered."

Tanya frowned.

"In addition, and most significant," the woman went on, "no burials of pharaohs are known to have taken place in the area you have described. However—"

"Yeah," Tanya shot back, "no known burials!"

Her father put a hand on her shoulder. "Tanya, calm down. Dr. Hagatha is only trying to help."

Dr. Hagatha wrinkled her brow as she peered closely at the pictures once again. "These are interesting photographs," she said, "but how you got them, or how they were taken in the first place . . . well, that I have no answer for."

Tanya rolled her eyes in frustration and her face became flushed. "You're like all the others," she blurted. "You don't believe me! No one does!"

"Control yourself, Tanya," her father said sternly.

"I'm sorry," Dr. Hagatha began, "if I gave you the impres—"

"Somehow I have to make people understand," Tanya interrupted. "I've got to make them believe me." She looked from Dr. Hagatha to her father. She wiped away a single tear coursing down her cheek.

"Young lady," Dr. Hagatha said in a kind voice, "I'd like to speak to your father alone for a moment." She smiled. "Why don't you go to the restroom and freshen up, and then we'll talk some more, okay?"

Her jaw clenched, Tanya got up and made her way from the office. But instead of going to the restroom she headed immediately downstairs. She had to prove she was telling the truth, reveal what she had discovered, and show the world the magic—and the mystery—of time. And she knew exactly how to do it.

In the street, in front of the university, a battered salmon-colored cab was waiting for her. This time Tanya was not at all surprised. She got into the cab. The driver nodded and headed in the direction Tanya indicated.

* * *

Frantic with worry, Isaac Fields went to the police. All of Cairo was searched, and then the search was expanded to outlying districts. A week passed, and then two, with no trace of Tanya. Isaac Fields went to the American Embassy, then to a private detective agency. The weeks turned into months.

Meanwhile Dr. Hagatha was able to convince the university to undertake an immediate excavation at Al-Matariyah. True, she had been skeptical when she had first heard Tanya's story and seen her photographs. Still, she had been intrigued, and she had been far more interested in pursuing the matter than she was able to convey to Tanya before the teenager had run away.

Day after day Dr. Hagatha was at Al-Matariyah, at the site of the excavation, overseeing the work. At first, Isaac Fields spent most of his time in his hotel room, constantly calling the police, the embassy, and the detective agency. But no one could offer any information about his missing daughter. Tanya, it seemed, had disappeared off the face of the earth. In despair, nearly abandoning all hope, he began spending more and more time at Al-Matariyah with Dr. Hagatha, watching the massive excavation his daughter's strange story had set into motion.

Dr. Hagatha's camp was on a low, rocky plateau overlooking Al-Matariyah. While she studied drawings and diagrams at a table set up outside her tent, conferred with other archaeologists, or toured the site in her Jeep, Isaac Fields usually sat in silence. He knew that he would never see Tanya again. Still, being near the place that had so captivated his daughter's imagination somehow made him feel closer to her.

One morning, a little after 10:00 A.M., Isaac Fields arrived at the camp. The temperature was already soaring past one hundred degrees. As usual, he greeted Dr. Hagatha, then sat down in the shade of her tent and quietly watched the work proceeding below.

Dr. Hagatha asked him if there had been any news of Tanya's whereabouts. When he shook his head as he always did, she offered him a few comforting and encouraging words, then returned to work.

Standing on a sandstone outcropping, she studied the

scene below. Everywhere, bulldozers hauled away heaps of trash and dug, clawed, and rumbled away with great scoops of sand. At the same time manual laborers toiled with picks, shovels, and hoes. Already some remnants of the ancient city of Iunu had been unearthed. Still, no trace whatsoever had been found of the burial vault Tanya had described.

Swatting at flies, her brow wet with perspiration, Dr. Hagatha watched as the workers dug deeper and deeper into the sand. But though her eyes were fixed on the workmen, her thoughts were elsewhere. Her mind kept returning to the day so many weeks ago when Tanya had nervously told her bizarre story.

Was the girl crazy? Dr. Hagatha wondered. *And am I also crazy for having ordered this excavation?*

Suddenly excited cries rose from the workmen.

"We have found it!" shouted a man in a nearby sector of the excavation. He and a half dozen other men began frantically brushing sand from a large doorlike slab of stone in the face of a half-buried octagon-shaped structure.

Dr. Hagatha and Isaac Fields picked their way down an embankment, then hurried across the sand to where the workmen were chipping away at an ancient resin seal. Then, with all their strength, the men—along with Dr. Hagatha and Isaac Fields—slowly wrestled with the huge door until it opened with a thunderous bang.

Everyone stood back in awe. Before them was the yawning entrance to a tunnellike chamber from which hot, centuries-old air escaped. Snatching up a flashlight, Dr. Hagatha, with Isaac Fields close behind, entered the dark, musty-smelling tunnel. Breathlessly they moved deeper and deeper down the dark passageway.

After a short while, they came to a stone stairway. Slowly, with Dr. Hagatha still in the lead, they made their way down until they came upon a pitch-black chamber. As their eyes adjusted to the darkness, and as Dr. Hagatha moved the beam of the flashlight about, details of the room emerged slowly in the gloom. The light revealed strange animal carvings, statues, jewelry, and a sarcophagus of gold.

"It's overwhelming," Dr. Hagatha whispered, her voice echoing off the dark stone walls.

"Is this the tomb Tanya photographed?" Isaac Fields whispered back. "Is it possible?"

Dr. Hagatha said nothing. She was walking ahead of him, gazing about in awe. She stepped closer to the golden sarcophagus, the beam of her flashlight playing eerily around the room. Suddenly it swept past a shadowy form. Dr. Hagatha steadied the beam of the light, then gasped.

"No!" Isaac Fields screamed, sinking to his knees.

The two of them stared in horror. Beside the long, intricately decorated sarcophagus lay a body. It was the mummified body of a teenage girl, a girl who had been dead for thousands of years, a girl with a camera around her neck and a remnant of a piece of paper clutched tightly in her withered hands.

Weeping, Isaac Fields took the piece of paper from his daughter's clenched fist. *Visit the ancient city of Iunu,* it said. *Enjoy the wonders of the past.*

THE HOUSE NEXT DOOR

*T*he old school bus rumbled through the streets of Farristown as it carried a load of noisy kids home. The new kid in school, Zeke Kimball, heard a squeaky-voiced girl sitting a few rows back use the same word over and over. The word was *ghouls*.

"What's she talking about?" Zeke asked Lamont Jones, who was sitting next to him. "What are ghouls?"

Lamont looked at him with surprise. "Man, haven't you heard about the ghouls here in Farristown? It's on every TV station."

Zeke looked at his shoes. "We don't have a TV," he admitted. "And my parents don't get the newspapers. We don't even have a radio."

"How come, man?"

"My parents just think the media is a bad influence. You know, 'cause of all the violence and bad language." Zeke shrugged, feeling embarrassed. "Everybody at school thinks I'm sort of lame."

"Well," Lamont said, "it *is* kind of weird, but I suppose it's not your fault if that's the way your parents are. I mean, my folks are strict, and I gotta pretty much do what they say, but no TV!" He ran a hand through his dark curly hair. "Now, *that's* got to be tough."

"Anyway," Zeke said, quickly changing the subject, "so what *are* ghouls?"

"They're kind of like cannibals," Lamont explained, "but they don't care if the people they eat just died or if they've been dead a hundred years."

"That's sick." Zeke wrinkled his nose in disgust. "You've got to be putting me on."

"It's true," Lamont insisted. "And it's been all over the news about how we've got some ghouls living right here in Farristown. Two kids disappeared a couple of weeks ago. And last night somebody dug up a grave in the cemetery and stole the body."

"Yuck!" Zeke exclaimed.

Lamont nodded his head gravely. "Yeah, the newspaper said they found the coffin near Three Fork River. And it was empty."

"Wow!" Zeke gasped, his eyes wide.

Lamont craned his neck out the window as the bus slowed on his block. "My stop is next. Wanna get off here and come over to my house for a while?"

"Thanks," Zeke said, then let out a heavy sigh. "Wish I could, but my parents wouldn't allow it." He rolled his eyes. "It's straight to school, then straight home."

"How about weekends?" Lamont suggested, gathering up his school books. "Tomorrow's Saturday, and—"

"Sometimes my parents let me go to the park to play baseball and stuff," Zeke said sadly, "but that's about it."

Lamont shook his head. "Hey, that's too bad, man," he said sympathetically. "But hey, give me your number anyway. I'll call you up and see if we can get together sometime."

"We don't have a phone," Zeke said flatly.

"You're lyin'," said Lamont, his mouth dropping open in disbelief. "Look, if you don't want to be friends, just say so."

"Sure, I do," Zeke said. "I—"

But the bus came to a stop, and Lamont hurried off without looking back.

Zeke sagged against his seat. As the bus lumbered away he silently wished that he were back in the orphanage or that different parents had adopted him.

* * *

Later that evening at supper Zeke just picked at his food.

"What's the matter, honey?" his mom asked.

His dad looked concerned, too. "You okay, sport?" He gave Zeke a friendly pat on the back.

Zeke looked up from his plate. "It's the way we live," he finally confessed. "Everybody thinks I'm an oddball. I mean, the most modern thing we own is a toaster. How come everyone else has a TV, a VCR, and about a hundred video games? We don't have anything." His voice rose so that he was practically yelling. "Not even a phone!"

His mother shook her head. "Now, Zeke, you know full well why we choose to live the way we do. If it makes us seem odd to other people just because we live simply and cleanly, then we prefer to be odd."

His dad put his hand on Zeke's shoulder. "Son, it's not as though we aren't sympathetic. Your mom and I understand how strong peer pressure can be, especially for a boy your age. It's very natural for you to want to fit in and be like everybody else."

"Yes, Dad," Zeke said, "I *do* want to be like the other kids. I want to know what's going on in the world. I mean, take today in my social studies class, for example. We were having a discussion about a famous murder trial going on in San Francisco, but I didn't even know what the teacher was talking about. And on the way home on the bus, the kids were talking about these ghouls that stole some bodies."

"Zeke," his mother interrupted him. "This is exactly the type of thing we want to avoid." She laughed. "I mean, really. *Ghouls!*"

"You mean it isn't true?" Zeke asked.

"I'd sincerely doubt it," his dad said. "It sounds like just the kind of stuff kids make up all the time. After a while, they begin to believe it."

Zeke didn't know if he was more relieved to find out the stories were phony or more embarrassed to find out he'd been stupid enough to believe them. He glanced at his mom and saw the warm, knowing look in her eyes. He could see she understood how he felt. She smiled and gave him a pat on the arm. "Now, eat your dinner before it gets cold, sweetheart," she said. "Then it's early to bed, early to rise."

"Makes a man healthy, wealthy, and wise," Zeke said, finishing the old saying he'd heard a billion times. "I know, I know." Then he forced a smile on his face and made himself clean his plate.

After dinner, Zeke and his dad played chess. Winning two games in a row really put Zeke in the mood for more. But then he noticed the time. It was almost eight o'clock, time for bed.

His dad put the chess set away. "We'll play again tomorrow, champ. But try to go a little easier on me, okay?" he added with a laugh.

"I'll try," Zeke mumbled, trudging off to his room and shutting the door.

The other kids already made fun of Zeke, but they would probably laugh their heads off if they found out how early he had to go to bed. After all, he was almost fourteen. At least he could read until nine, if he wanted, but after that he was not allowed to leave his room, even for a glass of water. Once it was lights-out, it was lights-out, and that was that.

Now, lying in bed, Zeke kept thinking about Lamont. He seemed like such a nice guy. *Maybe if I talk to him,* Zeke thought, *I'll be able to make him understand that it isn't my fault my parents are the way they are.*

Wide awake and feeling lonely, Zeke lay with his hands clasped behind his head, staring up at the ceiling.

And then the sounds began.

First he heard his parents lock up and head to their room. Then the cicadas started up, and in the distance he could hear the train rumbling by on the outskirts of town.

But those were just the *normal* night sounds.

It was about ten when all the weird sounds started happening. The noise came from right next door. Zeke had never met the people who lived there, but they sure were noisy, especially on weekends. And there were all sorts of strange goings-on, like cars coming and going at all hours of the night and people tromping around carrying huge bags of something.

Kneeling on his bed, he peeked out the window. Behind the drawn shades of the rundown white stucco house strange, ghostly shadows were moving about. Music was blaring, too. And was it his imagination, or did he see an upraised knife in the hand of one of the shadows?

Suddenly a low, cackling laugh erupted from one of the shadows, and something fell over with a bang. There was a muffled scream, followed by more laughter.

"What in the world is going on over there?" Zeke mumbled to himself.

And then he thought back to what Lamont had said about ghouls. Maybe his parents were wrong. Maybe it wasn't just a bunch of nonsense. Maybe the ghouls did exist and they lived next door!

Ugly visions began crawling around in Zeke's head, and in his mind's eye he imagined fanged monsters next door, laughing as they scarfed down a bunch of dead bodies.

As if on cue, raucous laughter erupted once again from across the way, and the music was turned up. Then suddenly Zeke heard what seemed like a cry for help.

Instantly the music went off, and Zeke spotted someone peeking out a broken window from behind a drape. The drape abruptly closed and all was silent for a moment. Then Zeke heard another weird noise coming from inside the house. It sounded like something heavy, perhaps a body, being dragged down from the attic. It made a thumping noise, as though it were being dragged downstairs and the head was bumping on each step. The sound kept stopping and starting, as if the body were heavy and whoever was dragging it needed to stop from time to time to rest.

His nerves on edge, Zeke saw a light go on in the room directly across from him. The dragging sound started again, and another shadow passed behind the drawn shade of a window. Then came a *whoosh* and a *bang*, like the sound of a heavy door being closed. An eerie silence followed as Zeke continued to watch.

Suddenly there was a sharp knock on his bedroom door, and Zeke almost jumped out of his skin.

"Hope I didn't startle you, honey," his mom said, poking her head into his room.

"Well, maybe just a little," Zeke admitted. He shuddered. "Something weird is going on in that house again tonight."

His mom pulled her flannel robe around herself against the chill. "I know. We heard it, too. It was keeping both your dad and me awake."

"Especially on weekend nights, all sorts of weird stuff starts up over there," Zeke said. "And sometimes I see cars come and go late at night, but I never see the people out in their yard during the day or even see them leave for work in the morning."

"Well, I'm going to the police if this keeps up," said his dad, who had just walked into Zeke's room. "Live and let live, I always say. But we have a right to peace and quiet!"

"Dad," Zeke began hesitantly, "do you think it's possible ghouls live over there? I mean, after hearing all that stuff today—"

"Son," his Dad interrupted, "the people next door are very loud and inconsiderate, but that's *all*. I don't like to

112

see you getting all worked up because of stupid stories that kids make up. Okay, sport?"

Zeke nodded.

His mom scuffled over in her carpet slippers, tucked Zeke in, and gave him a kiss. "Get some rest, darling," she said, giving him a loving wink.

But as soon as his parents were out of the room, Zeke went back to watching the house next door. Something was going on over there, and he was going to figure out what it was.

* * *

At school on Monday Lamont seemed to be trying to avoid Zeke. But finally, by the end of the day, Zeke was able to have a talk with him and convince him that he hadn't lied about not having a phone. All week the two boys hung around together at lunchtime and usually sat together on the bus on the way home. On Friday Zeke invited Lamont to come over to his house on Saturday.

"Yeah," Lamont said thoughtfully. "I guess if your folks won't let you come over to my house, I could come over to yours." He grinned. "Then I'll see for myself that you don't have a TV or a phone."

On Saturday morning Zeke woke up in a great mood. He helped his dad in the garage for a while, then went to the market with his mom. All he could talk about was how his buddy Lamont was coming over.

But Lamont never showed.

Zeke's mom looked terribly worried. "Maybe he got the address wrong," she suggested.

"Or maybe," his dad offered, "he came by when you and your mom went to the market. I was in the garage working and I wouldn't have heard him."

"It's nice of you to try to cheer me up," Zeke said, shrugging. "But I just don't seem to be able to make friends very well."

Zeke spent the rest of the weekend moping. And when he went to school on Monday, he didn't want to talk to anybody, especially Lamont Jones.

But as it turned out, that was not a problem. Lamont wasn't in class on Monday, and the rumor around school was that the ghouls got him. Zeke dismissed the idea as just more baloney. But that night two police officers, Detectives Carmine Kennedy and John Sandoval, came to talk to Zeke and his parents.

"As we understand it," Detective Sandoval said, "Lamont Jones was your friend."

"Yeah, sort of," Zeke said. "Is he all right?"

"Lamont disappeared on Saturday," Detective Kennedy said, pausing. "And we were told by his mother that the last time she saw him he was leaving to come to your house."

"Coming to my house?" Zeke's mouth dropped open. "Oh, Mom! Dad!" Zeke cried. "That means—"

Detective Sandoval raised an eyebrow. "Means what, son?"

But Zeke was too distraught to continue, so his mom explained how Zeke had waited all day for Lamont and how upset he'd been when his friend hadn't shown up.

"Do you think the boy was kidnapped?" Zeke's father asked gravely.

"Right now, Mr. Kimball, we're exploring every possibility." Detective Kennedy flipped through her notebook. "But I'm afraid right now we don't have any leads."

Zeke looked at the floor, lost in thought.

"And you're sure," Detective Kennedy asked as she put a hand on Zeke's shoulder, "that your friend never showed up here?"

"No, he didn't," Zeke's father said, answering for him. He frowned and looked at both detectives. "What kind of a world are we living in, Officers? What kind of world is it when a child isn't safe just walking over to a friend's house to play?"

* * *

Zeke ran up to his room in tears as soon as the detectives left. Soon afterward, his parents came in to talk to him.

"Let's just think good thoughts," his mom suggested.

"And hope your friend turns up alive and well," his dad added.

Zeke buried his face in his pillow. "Yeah, right,"

His dad gave him a pat on the back. "We know you're upset, Zeke. But this, too, shall pass."

"Now, brush your teeth and get into your pajamas, honey," his mom said. "I'll come tuck you in when you're ready."

The door shut softly as his parents left the room.

Thinking about Lamont, Zeke fell asleep in his clothes, his head full of dark, ugly thoughts. He rolled over groggily sometime later, feeling someone put a warm quilt over him. With one sleepy eye opened, he caught a glimpse of his mom turning off his light, then tiptoeing out of the room. Then, just before he drifted back to sleep, he saw the luminous dials of the clock by his bed and checked the time. It was 11:34.

The room was cold when Zeke woke again. Forcing himself awake out of a horrifying nightmare filled with ghouls, he was drenched in a cold sweat and his stomach was in knots. Startled, he sat up in bed and glanced at the clock again. It was almost 3:00 A.M.

He was nauseated. Not only was he sick with fear, he felt as though he might be coming down with the flu. Throwing the quilt aside, he looked at the closed door. He knew he wasn't allowed to leave the room, but this was sort of an emergency.

Mom and Dad will understand if I leave just this once to get them, he thought. *They wouldn't want me to stay in here and not tell them if I think I'm sick.*

Putting his bathrobe on over his clothes against the cold, he hurried from his room and down the hall.

"Mom! Dad!" he called, knocking on their bedroom door.

When there was no answer, he knocked again. Then, after turning the knob, he peered in and stared in disbelief. No one was there.

Calling for his parents and clutching his aching stomach, Zeke wandered through the dark house. Finding no trace of them, he returned to his parents' room. It was eerie and lit by the moon. As he looked around he noticed something was wrong. At first he didn't know what it was. Then he realized that the built-in bookcase was slightly ajar. He walked over and pulled on it, then swung it open to find a long descending stairway behind the wall.

Breaking into a cold sweat again, he crept down the stairs and then found himself walking along a passageway. It made an abrupt turn, ascended slightly, then ended in front of a heavy warped door.

He turned the knob and was astonished to find himself stepping into what appeared to be a kitchen. It was dark and littered with debris. And there was a moldy, rotten smell in the air.

Finding a window, Zeke pushed back a set of dusty curtains—and gaped in horror. His eyes wide and the hair standing up on the back of his neck, he realized that he was staring at his own house across the way! That meant he was *in* the house next door!

Zeke wanted to run screaming back home, but behind him, coming from upstairs, he heard the sound of muffled voices. His heart pounding, he followed the voices, slowly taking the steps one at a time toward the door at the top of the stairs. The horrid odor was becoming stronger with each step, and the muffled voices were becoming louder.

"Get rid of every scrap of evidence," hissed a voice.

"I'm too full," someone said with a giggle.

Zeke wanted to scream, to cry, to run. But how could he? They might hear him. Quietly he tried to ease back down the dark stairs when suddenly he tripped over something. It was the jacket that Lamont always wore! Horrified, he started to scream, but a hand clamped over his mouth from behind.

"Shouldn't stick your nose in where it doesn't belong," someone with a familiar voice said.

Slowly Zeke turned and found himself face-to-face with his father.

"We told you to stay in your room," his mother scolded, stepping out of the shadows behind Zeke's dad. "You disobeyed us."

"You've created a terrible quandary for us," his father

said. "We really *do* care for you, but we also have our own lives, our own needs."

"Mom! Dad! How could you?" Zeke blurted out. He was paralyzed with fear and disbelief.

His father chuckled, then shrugged. "To each his own," he said.

"Different strokes for different folks," his mother added, throwing her hands up.

Zeke took a halting step backward. Then he turned to run. But strong arms grabbed hold of him.

* * *

A week later Detectives Kennedy and Sandoval again showed up at the Kimball's front door. They wanted to know if Zeke's parents had any new information, anything at all, that might help them in their search for Lamont Jones.

"Nothing," Zeke's father said.

"How about your son?" Detective Kennedy asked. "Does he know anything?"

"We sent Zeke to live with his grandparents in Utah. With a kidnapper running loose in our town, we just couldn't take any chances."

"Maybe we're just old worrywarts," Zeke's mom added, a bowl of cookie batter in her hands. "But we are firm believers in—"

"No, ma'am," Detective Sandoval said. "You're right to be careful. I wish more parents were like you."

"How true," said Zeke's father, nodding wisely. "We *all* have to be a little more careful these days."

SO GOOD TO BE HOME

It was just a routine spacebus flight. Paul and his buddy Henry were on their way home from a summer vacation at the boys' camp on the planet Tantalus, when suddenly there was a horrid cracking noise coming from somewhere in the spacebus.

"What's that?" Paul asked Henry, who was startled out of a nap.

"I don't know," Henry said.

Just then yellow oxygen masks shot out from the backs of the seats in front of them. "Something's happening," Paul said, struggling with one of the masks to get it properly adjusted over his face. Henry, his eyes wide with fear, just sat there.

"Come on, man," Paul said, handing his friend the other mask. "Put it on."

The flight attendant yelled for everyone to be calm. Over the intercom the pilot began telling them to prepare for an emergency landing. Henry numbly did as he was told. Then the craft, which had been lurching from side to side, steadied itself as it glided in slow descent.

Paul looked at Henry, still in near shock. "It's okay, buddy," Paul said as everyone breathed a collective sigh of relief and began talking amongst themselves through the mouthpieces in their oxygen masks. "Look, everyone's calming down. Nothing's going to happen."

"We will be making a landing on an uninhabited planet," the captain suddenly announced over the intercom. "It is not listed on any of the maps, but I will contact galactic control and tell them our position. Our communications systems are presently down, but I will restore power and make contact as soon—"

But all of a sudden the captain's steady voice turned into a scream. Paul looked at Henry, who had begun crying and pointing toward the front of the spacebus. Following the line of Henry's finger, Paul saw something that froze his heart. The cockpit was in flames. He was about to burst into tears himself when a huge *whoompf* sounded overhead, followed by the grinding sound of metal being torn apart.

In horror, Paul threw his hands over his face. Then slowly he managed to look around. He saw nothing but purple-blue space! He cautiously tilted his head back to confirm his worst fear. The roof of the spacebus had come off and had been sucked out into space. If not for his seat belt, Paul would have met the same fate.

"Help me!" the flight attendant began shrieking as she desperately gripped the headrest of the seat across from Paul. But before he had a chance to even think of what to do, the young woman flew right out of the top of the bus. Rapidly she became miniaturized by distance. Looking like a small, screaming doll being sucked into space, she wailed "Noooooooooo!" until her voice was only a faint echo.

Just then a powerful wind raced through the bus like a tornado, sending plastic cups, luggage, and pieces of the spacecraft swirling around the cabin. Paul turned to grab hold of Henry, to find comfort in his friend and to offer his own support. Instead he was stunned by a terrible sight.

"Henry?" Paul gazed at his friend in disbelief.

Henry's eyes stared blankly. A jagged metal bar had pinned him to the seat, crushing him.

Gasping, Paul looked away from his dead friend. Other passengers were dead, too, bombarded by flying objects. A few still strapped to their seats like Paul stared straight ahead, waiting to die. It was like riding in a huge convertible, only they were deep in outer space, not safe on the ground. And they weren't drifting toward home. They were drifting down toward an empty planet.

The spacebus rolled over a few times and was now flying upside down. Suddenly all of the seats on the left side ripped away as a single unit from the floor. Paul stared in terror and amazement at what looked like a metal roller-coaster filled with horrified thrill seekers zooming away into the dark sky. Like the poor flight attendant, both their bodies and their screams soon miniaturized into nothingness.

Then, to Paul's relief, the spacebus righted itself and appeared to be drifting gently downward. But an instant later it began to flip end-over-end and slammed into the face of the unknown planet with a thunderous roar.

* * *

The next thing Paul knew, flames were licking around him. *I've got to get out of here,* his mind raced, amazed he was even alive to think. With blood streaming down his face, he struggled to get out of the twisted wreckage.

"Help me!" he heard someone cry.

And then he saw a girl stumbling toward him through a haze of smoke in the wrecked bus. Quickly he made his way toward her. Then, the second he reached her, she fainted in his arms.

"Hang on," he said. And with every bit of strength he had left, Paul pulled himself and the unconscious girl through a jagged hole in the side of the bus. He had just dragged her as far as he could, about twenty yards, when the entire spacebus exploded. Then something hit him from behind, and he went reeling into unconsciousness.

* * *

When Paul came to, he found himself lying next to the girl he had rescued. "Are you okay?" he asked. But when he looked at her unseeing eyes, he knew she was anything but okay. She was dead.

He stared emptily at the spacebus, now nothing but a smoking skeleton of metal. *Am I the only survivor?* he asked himself, and then he called out, "Is anyone else alive?"

But no one answered. Overcome with pain from his own cuts and burns, and stricken with terror and grief, Paul fell to his knees and sobbed.

He knew that he, too, would soon be dead. There was no way off the planet. And there was no hope of being rescued. He remembered how the captain had said the spacebus's communications systems were down. Besides, the cockpit had gone up in flames before the captain could have reported the bus's position. Now it lay in pieces on an unknown planet, thousands of light-years from Earth. No one, no one in the entire universe even knew of the crash, let alone where Paul was. He was sure of it.

"Help me!" Paul cried out to no one, certain he would never see home, his parents, or his sister again. "Please, if anyone is out there, help me!"

Panicking, Paul dragged himself to his feet. Then turning in a circle, he gazed past the smoking wreckage. As far as the eye could see there was nothing. The surface of the planet appeared to be no more than an endless slab of smooth marble. There wasn't a tree, a river, or a hill. It seemed nothing lived, nothing grew, and not a breath of wind stirred across the empty landscape.

He began to walk, often slipping and falling. Each time, he listlessly picked himself up and kept going. He didn't really have a clue why, and he didn't really care.

After about an hour, Paul began to weaken. The pain from his cuts and burns became steadily worse with each step, sapping his last bit of strength. "Why should I keep going?" he asked himself. "There's nothing here."

But that's when he saw something. In the near distance was a pedestal of some kind.

Instantly a faint spark of hope stirred within him. Drawn to the object as if by some unseen force, he lumbered toward it, growing more excited, and more afraid, with each step. His heart pounding, his eyes growing wide with horror, he approached the pedestal . . . and the monstrosity on top of it.

"What is it?" he gasped, wanting to run away. But driven by curiosity and desperation, he stepped closer.

Standing right in front of the pedestal now, Paul stared at what was on top of it in revulsion and disbelief. It appeared to be a basket of red, green, and black veins encased in an oversized head of transparent skin and bone.

"Are you afraid?" the thing asked, its strange-looking opaque eyes blinking in their sockets embedded in the see-through skull.

Too horrified to answer, Paul stared in dumbstruck awe.

"You are from Earth?" the thing asked.

"Yes, I—I'm from Earth," Paul stammered. "But how did you know?"

In response, a cryptic smile formed on the thing's face, but no words came from its mouth.

"What are you?" Paul asked, growing braver, for so far no harm had come to him and the thing didn't seem hostile. He looked around at the desolate landscape, in search of more pedestals, of more heads, but saw nothing. "Are there more, uh, creatures like you?"

"No," the thing responded sadly. "I am alone."

"How did you come to be here?" asked Paul.

"It is my punishment. I have been here since before the beginning of time as you know it, and I shall remain here forever." The thing paused, as if letting Paul digest what it had said. "I am from the other side of what you call the universe," it went on. "Somewhere you Earthlings have not explored."

"Why are you here? And how did you get here?" Paul asked. He seemed to suddenly have a million questions.

The brain inside the transparent skull turned a dark color, as though distressed by its own thoughts and memories. "I was banished from my world for opposing its leaders and questioning the correctness of their thoughts. I was exiled here for eternity, placed here on this column of stone to reexamine my own thinking. And I shall do so forever, for in my world there is no end to life."

"You mean you can't die?" asked Paul incredulously. "You mean there's no such thing as death?"

The mouth on the head frowned. "For me there is only the eternal agony of being alone with my own thoughts. I am so very lonely, and I am so pleased to have you here with me. So very pleased to have you for some company." The liquidy eyes looked Paul up and down. "You are hurt and in pain. I do not wish my new companion to suffer."

In wonderment Paul stared at his hands and legs. His pain had miraculously vanished. He quickly touched his face. His burns had disappeared, too!

"How did you do that?" Paul asked, astonished.

"I can do anything," the thing responded, and smiled as a hand and arm grew from the pedestal, complete with bony fingers that reached out and touched Paul's face tenderly.

Sickened by the creature's touch, Paul screamed and jumped back. "I have to go," he said, trying to stay calm. "We're different. I don't mean to offend you, but I want to be with my own kind."

"Don't leave!" the creature ordered. "Stay with me!"

But Paul turned to run anyway.

"Please," the creature begged. "I am lonely."

Terrified, Paul began to take off when he suddenly found himself screaming and falling in agony to the ground. In horror, he realized that both his legs were broken.

"I can hurt you if I wish," the creature thundered. "And I can make you afraid!"

Suddenly a shark swam through the air at Paul, opening a mouth full of serrated teeth. Unable to run with his broken legs, he put his hands out to defend himself against the shark.

"I can make whatever causes your fear to go away, as well," the creature shouted. "And I can rid you of your pain if I so choose."

And with that the shark shrank to a dot, then disappeared. Baffled, Paul stumbled to his feet, his broken legs instantly healed.

"Are you happy now?" the creature asked.

Not knowing what else to do, Paul nodded.

"Look behind you," the creature commanded. "See? I can make you even happier."

Slowly Paul turned around and there, standing in front of him, was his mother!

"Mom!" he cried, running to embrace her. She was the most welcome individual he could have imagined. But just as his arms closed around her, she crumbled to dust. Then a breeze from nowhere blew up, carrying away the dust that had been his mother.

"What are you doing?" Paul shrieked, rushing toward the hideous head. "Why are you torturing me?!"

"Stop!" the creature ordered.

Paul had just reached the ugly neck of the thing and was about to crush it when his hands burst into flames. Falling back in agony, he rolled over and over on the ground. "Please!" he cried. "Please, stop the pain!"

"It's only in your mind," the creature said calmly. "You stop it."

"But I can't!" Paul screeched. "It's so real!"

"I know," the creature said matter-of-factly.

And then the fire vanished.

"What's happening?" Paul asked, slowly rising to his feet. Suddenly he found himself in his own bedroom. Amazed, he walked around the room, picked up his football, touched the posters on his wall, then riffled through the papers and other junk on his desk. Yes, it was *his* desk. He was in *his* room.

Then a phone rang.

"I'll get it," his sister called from the other room just as he was reaching for the extension on his desk. *It's true!* he thought. *I'm home! It was all just a dream.*

And then the phone disappeared, and so did his room. And there was Paul again, alone with the strange creature, alone on the barren planet.

"I wish you wanted to stay with me," the thing said, pausing as if thinking.

"No!" Paul cried. "I *really* want to be at home!"

"But you can never go," the creature replied. "I want you to stay here." The mouth on the transparent face attempted to smile. "Still, I can give you all you desire. I can make you *feel* like you are home."

"What do you want with me?" Paul asked helplessly. "If you are so powerful, why won't you give me back my home for real?"

"Because I am alone. Because with you here with me I will be happy." The creature looked at Paul with true affection. "But don't worry. At the same time I can give you what you desire most. Go now . . . go into your mind. Be happy. You shall never see me again."

And with that Paul found himself back in his bedroom.

He walked to the window and pressed his face against the cold, wet glass, looking down at the street below. A misty rain, illuminated in the glow of streetlights, was falling. For a long time he just stood and watched, dumbfounded.

Across the way his neighbor, Mrs. Donaldson, went hurrying up the walkway to her house. As she fumbled with her keys a light went on inside the house and someone opened the door for her. Then it shut with a bang, which started the dog barking down the street.

It all seemed so normal, so real. But it wasn't. Paul knew that the thing, the head on the pedestal, was creating all this within his mind.

He touched the cold glass of the window, gazing at his reflection. He knew that he was inside of his mind, while his body was really on another planet, somewhere in another galaxy. But it was getting harder and harder now to keep everything clear. It was becoming difficult even to remember what had happened to him. The crash, the transparent head, even the fear, all seemed to fade, to speed backward into some dark corner of his subconscious. Then suddenly all those things were gone, lost far beyond the reach of his memory.

And he was home. To feel, to believe, or to think anything else was now impossible.

His mom walked into the room.

Paul smiled and he ran to her.

It was so good, so wonderful, to be home.